WAR CRY!

"Iiiieeeeaaaaa!"

The Viking's war cry split the still air. He brandished the huge ax above his head, his massive arms barely straining with the weight, his well-muscled legs pounding the earth like big pistons. The man's blond hair and long, full beard waved wildly, and his blue eyes, barely visible under the visor of his iron helmet, blazed with lust for combat as he charged.

"Look out!" Joe yelled to his brother.

The Viking charged between them and aimed the ax at Frank's head. . . .

Books in THE HARDY BOYS CASEFILES™ Series

#1 DEAD ON TARGET
#2 EVIL, INC.
#3 CULT OF CRIME
#4 THE LAZARUS PLOT
#5 EDGE OF DESTRUCTION
#6 THE CROWNING TERROR
#7 DEATHGAME
#8 SEE NO EVIL
#9 THE GENIUS THIEVES
#12 PERFECT GETAWAY
#13 THE BORGIA DAGGER
#14 TOO MANY TRAITORS
#29 THICK AS THIEVES
#30 THE DEADLIEST DARE
#32 BLOOD MONEY
#33 COLLISION COURSE
#35 THE DEAD SEASON
#37 DANGER ZONE
#41 HIGHWAY ROBBERY
#42 THE LAST LAUGH
#44 CASTLE FEAR
#45 IN SELF-DEFENSE
#46 FOUL PLAY
#47 FLIGHT INTO DANGER
#48 ROCK 'N' REVENGE
#49 DIRTY DEEDS
#50 POWER PLAY
#52 UNCIVIL WAR
#53 WEB OF HORROR
#54 DEEP TROUBLE
#55 BEYOND THE LAW
#56 HEIGHT OF DANGER
#57 TERROR ON TRACK
#60 DEADFALL
#61 GRAVE DANGER
#62 FINAL GAMBIT
#63 COLD SWEAT
#64 ENDANGERED SPECIES
#65 NO MERCY
#66 THE PHOENIX EQUATION
#69 MAYHEM IN MOTION
#70 RIGGED FOR REVENGE
#71 REAL HORROR
#73 BAD RAP
#74 ROAD PIRATES
#75 NO WAY OUT
#76 TAGGED FOR TERROR
#77 SURVIVAL RUN
#78 THE PACIFIC CONSPIRACY
#79 DANGER UNLIMITED
#80 DEAD OF NIGHT
#81 SHEER TERROR
#82 POISONED PARADISE
#83 TOXIC REVENGE
#84 FALSE ALARM
#85 WINNER TAKE ALL
#86 VIRTUAL VILLAINY
#87 DEAD MAN IN DEADWOOD
#88 INFERNO OF FEAR
#89 DARKNESS FALLS
#90 DEADLY ENGAGEMENT
#91 HOT WHEELS
#92 SABOTAGE AT SEA
#93 MISSION: MAYHEM
#94 A TASTE FOR TERROR
#95 ILLEGAL PROCEDURE
#96 AGAINST ALL ODDS
#97 PURE EVIL
#98 MURDER BY MAGIC
#99 FRAME-UP
#100 TRUE THRILLER
#101 PEAK OF DANGER
#102 WRONG SIDE OF THE LAW
#103 CAMPAIGN OF CRIME
#104 WILD WHEELS
#105 LAW OF THE JUNGLE
#106 SHOCK JOCK
#107 FAST BREAK
#108 BLOWN AWAY
#109 MOMENT OF TRUTH
#115 CAVE TRAP
#116 ACTING UP
#117 BLOOD SPORT
#118 THE LAST LEAP
#119 THE EMPEROR'S SHIELD
#120 SURVIVAL OF THE FITTEST
#121 ABSOLUTE ZERO
#122 RIVER RATS
#123 HIGH-WIRE ACT
#124 THE VIKING'S REVENGE

Available from ARCHWAY Paperbacks

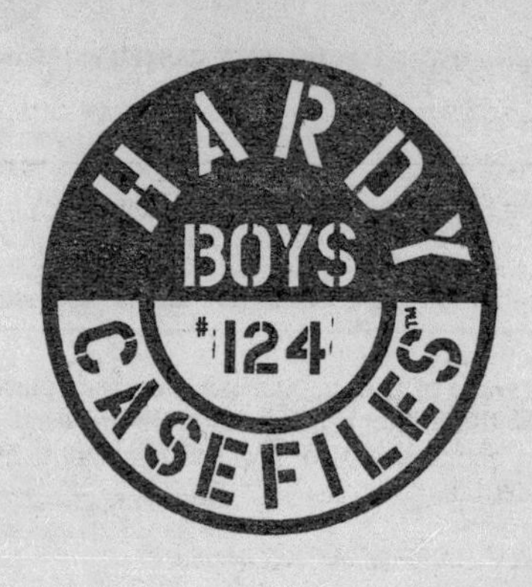

THE VIKING'S REVENGE

FRANKLIN W. DIXON

AN ARCHWAY PAPERBACK
Published by POCKET BOOKS
New York London Toronto Sydney Tokyo Singapore

This book is a work of fiction. Names, characters, places and incidents are products of the author's imagination or are used fictitiously. Any resemblance to actual events or locales or persons, living or dead, is entirely coincidental.

AN ARCHWAY PAPERBACK *Original*

An Archway Paperback published by
POCKET BOOKS, a division of Simon & Schuster Inc.
1230 Avenue of the Americas, New York, NY 10020

Produced by Mega-Books of New York, Inc.

ISBN: 0-671-56124-3

First Archway Paperback printing July 1997

10 9 8 7 6 5 4 3 2 1

Cover art by John Youssi

Printed in the U.S.A.

IL 6+

THE VIKING'S REVENGE

Chapter 1

"HEY, YOU! LET GO OF HIM!" Joe Hardy yelled as he leaped from the moving van.

Frank stomped on the brakes, and the squeal of tires shattered the stillness of a rainy, foggy summer afternoon. As soon as he had stopped the van, Frank bolted out the door after his brother.

The person choking the Hardys' friend Chet Morton spun around at the commotion. A large man, he was wearing a gray cloak with a hood that hid his face and made him look ghostlike. He and Chet were struggling on a path leading to the parking lot of Viking Village, a major tourist attraction near Burton, Minnesota.

Seeing the brothers charging, the attacker let go, and Chet fell to his knees, clutching his neck.

Before the Hardys could reach him, the attacker turned and ran into the nearby woods, quickly disappearing into the fog.

"Chet! Are you all right?" Joe asked, rushing to his friend's side.

Chet Morton got up slowly and took a few deep breaths. "Yeah. I'm okay," he said.

Frank sprinted past Chet and his brother and into the woods. Unfortunately, he couldn't see much, due to the fog and the dense tree cover. Pine needles blanketed the ground, so he couldn't even find any footprints. About twenty-five yards in, Frank realized his quarry had escaped, so he returned to the parking lot. "Lost him," he said, as he walked up to Chet and Joe.

"Well, this is a great way to start a summer vacation," Joe said. "What's going on, Chet? Any idea who that was?"

"Nope," Chet said. "I was just walking down the path to meet you guys when suddenly—*bam!*—the guy jumped me from behind. Imagine being mugged in this place." Chet had gotten a summer job at Viking Village.

"Did he take anything?" Frank asked.

Chet patted himself all over. "I don't think so. But he just about strangled me."

As they started to walk back toward the Hardys' van, Joe noticed that the main visitors' lot was nearly empty. That was probably due to the bad weather, he thought.

"I'll park, and we can get our stuff out," Joe said.

"Good idea," Frank said.

Joe hopped into the van, started it up, and pulled it into a parking spot. Then he got out, opened the back of the van, and began pitching luggage to Frank, who had walked over to the van, followed by Chet.

"Chet, has anything like this ever happened before?" Frank asked as he caught the bags.

"No," Chet said, but something in his voice made both Frank and Joe stop. Joe crossed his arms over his chest. Frank arched one dark eyebrow. At times like this, it was easy to tell the Hardys were brothers.

"Well," Chet said, shuffling his feet, "not to *me,* anyway. Let's go. I'll fill you in later. You guys must be tired." He motioned for the Hardys to follow him.

"You've got that right," Joe said, locking up the van. "We've been driving for three days." He and Frank fell into step with their friend.

"You'll be staying in my cabin," Chet said. "Construction on the guesthouses is behind schedule, so visitors stay in nearby motels. I got Mr. Trudson—he's the owner I told you about in my letter—to agree to let you stay in my cabin. You'll have to pay for your food, but he won't charge you to stay with me."

"Good thing, too, if we have to put up with your snoring," Frank said.

Chet led the Hardys to the main gate of the attraction. A sleepy-looking guard waved them past.

"Shouldn't you report what just happened?" Frank asked.

"I will, but old John isn't the one to report it to," Chet said. "We're supposed to tell the boss directly about any problems. We'll track him down as soon as I get you guys squared away."

They went through a passageway in an earthen rampart, or berm, and onto a boardwalk made out of logs. As they entered the village, they passed a gift shop hawking brightly colored Nordic souvenirs.

Before them Viking Village stretched downhill to the shores of Lake Superior. It was a re-creation of a traditional Viking settlement, with houses made of timber, stone, and sod. Smoke wafted into the summer air from holes in the roofs of several of the larger buildings.

To the west, through the mist, Frank could make out the mast of a longship moored at a pier on the lake. Log walks covered most of the attraction's major streets. The rest were dirt—mud actually, he thought, since it had rained recently. People dressed in Viking costumes strolled along the streets, mixing with tourists.

The earthen wall surrounded nearly the entire compound. A clinging mist made the entire village look mysterious, Joe thought, as if it had just materialized out of the distant past.

"That's a pretty impressive dirt wall," Joe said, indicating the berm.

"It was built to keep out enemies," Chet said. "Vikings had a lot of them, you know."

"Right now I'd be more interested in *your* enemies," Frank said. "Any ideas?"

"Not really," Chet said. "You guys know I'm pretty easygoing. I get along with almost everybody here. Maybe that attack was somebody's idea of horseplay. Vikings play pretty rough sometimes."

Joe frowned. He could see Chet was holding back. While he admired his friend's casual attitude, Joe found it frustrating to try to get information from Chet. "You said nothing like this had happened to *you* before. But that doesn't mean it hasn't happened to somebody else. Why don't you tell us what's up?"

As they turned left and headed downhill toward the dock area, Chet took a deep breath, then said, "Look, most of the other workers don't think there's anything to this, but I'm not so sure. Nobody else has been mugged, but some strange things have been happening around here lately. A few huts—that's what we call our cabins—have been ransacked, and some stuff was taken. Also, a few small artifacts have been stolen from the Visitor Center. Let me tell you, Trudson was upset about that. He runs a pretty tight ship."

"I'm not surprised you're having vandalism problems with such an alert guard at the gate,"

Joe said, hooking his thumb back toward the way they had come.

"John?" Chet said. "He's a retired policeman Mr. Trudson hired in case of emergencies. He's a good guy, but he's here mostly for show. He keeps the kids in line and makes the guests feel safer. It's a quiet place, really."

"I noticed a lot of the buildings aren't finished," Frank said.

"Yeah. We've been working on them in between our other duties, but it's slow going. I'm sure once we get the whole thing done, Mr. Trudson will hire more security. For now all the important stuff is kept locked up in the Visitor Center. After the thefts, he even put the small artifacts on display in locked cases. At night the center is fully alarmed."

They went out through the earthen wall and turned left into an area that was dotted with small cabins. Joe guessed this must be where the staff lived.

"Anything else?" Frank asked.

"Yeah, a couple of crazy accidents, too. Like my former cabin mate stepping in a hole and spraining his ankle. The hole wasn't there when we closed up the night before. I think somebody dug it on purpose, as a trap."

Frank smiled as he clapped his friend on the shoulder. "Well, if your roommate hadn't gone home, Joe and I wouldn't have anyplace to stay."

"Yeah," Joe said. "Bad luck for him. Good luck for you."

"Why? Because I get to share my cabin with you two overgrown adolescents?" Chet said. Joe chuckled. "So," Chet continued, "did you have any trouble finding the place?"

"Not too much," Frank said. "Although your handwriting was pretty hard to read."

"We would have had *less* trouble if Frank hadn't spilled coffee on the map and letter you sent us," Joe said.

"Which would you rather have, coffee stains or me asleep at the wheel?" Frank asked.

"Neither. If you had let me drive more—"

"I just wanted to get here in one piece," Frank said.

"Okay, guys, break it up," Chet said. "My hut's just up ahead. You can move the van out of the main lot to the staff lot later. It's closer. Ah! Here we are now. Home sweet hovel."

Chet pointed down the walkway, indicating a small wooden cabin with a thatched roof that stood in a pine grove amid a group of similar buildings.

Joe frowned. None of the huts looked very comfortable by twentieth-century standards. They were made of logs, thatch, sod, and stone. "That's the best you can do?" he asked.

Chet thumped his chest proudly. "Hey, in the village we live like Vikings. Vikings were tough—glad to have even a scrap of roof over their heads. They traveled all over the world and never complained. They even discovered America. That's what Mr. Trudson says, anyway."

Frank chuckled. "They also burned and looted half of Europe."

"Well," Chet said, "that's not what this place is about. We're trying to re-create the best parts of Viking living: the honor, the community, the sense of adventure. Mr. Trudson's gone to a lot of effort to make this a model Viking village. In fact, he only added the gift shop this season."

"Does that mean no indoor plumbing?" Joe asked.

"Nah. Don't worry, Joe. We *do* have bathrooms in the cabins. But the outsides are pretty authentic—to keep up appearances."

"Too bad," Frank said. "I was hoping we'd have to read by the light of an oil lamp."

Chet headed toward the door of his cabin. "Only if the power fails."

He put his hand on the door latch. Just then the cabin door swung open from the inside, and a young blond-haired woman wearing a traditional Viking costume darted out of the hut, nearly knocking Chet over. He caught her by the arms and held her face-to-face for a moment.

"Oh, Chet!" she exclaimed. "Thank goodness!"

"Ingrid," Chet said, "what are you doing here?" He let go of her and took a step back.

Ingrid looked all around. "I—I think someone was following me. I was on my break, taking a walk in the woods past the new longhouse. I heard something in the brush, but I didn't see anything, so I kept walking. But I kept feeling someone was watching me.

"Then I heard the noise in the brush again, closer this time. So I ran over here. When you weren't home, I guess I panicked a little. I decided I'd better find John. But when I pulled the door open, I ran into you." She smiled.

Chet put his arm around her and gave her a quick hug. "Don't worry," he said. "You're safe. These are my friends, Frank and Joe Hardy. Guys, this is Ingrid Lampford."

"Pleased to meet you, Ingrid," Frank said.

"Me, too," said Joe, shaking her hand enthusiastically. With her pale complexion, delicate features, and deep blue eyes, she was striking, Joe thought.

"You never saw anybody following you?" Frank asked.

"No. I just had this feeling."

"Why did you come all the way over to Chet's cabin?" Joe asked.

Ingrid looked from Chet to the Hardys and back again. "Who else would I come to?" she asked.

Chet chuckled nervously. "Sorry, guys. Guess I forgot to tell you in my letter. Ingrid and I are sort of . . . dating."

Frank and Joe tried not to show their surprise. Chet and Ingrid made an odd couple. Chet was a big, husky guy and not bad looking, but Ingrid was really stunning.

"Congratulations, Chet," Frank said.

"Yeah, Morton," Joe said. "So you were holding out on us." Chet grinned.

"Getting back to business," Joe said, turning to Ingrid "can you tell us anything else about this stalker?"

"Well," Ingrid said, "some other people have been followed, too. They said they'd seen . . ." She looked at Chet.

"I know you guys are going to laugh," Chet said, "but people are saying there's a real Viking lurking in the woods."

"A real Viking?" Joe scoffed. "Vikings don't exist anymore. Sounds like one of the workers is just playing a prank."

"I don't think so," Chet said. "We all know each other pretty well here. If it was one of the staff, somebody would have recognized him."

Ingrid cut in. "Some people say it's a *ghost* Viking."

"Why don't Joe and I check it out?" Frank suggested. "You two can wait here until we get back."

"Where exactly were you when you were being followed?" Joe asked Ingrid.

"In the woods on the north side of camp."

Chet gave Frank and Joe directions, and the Hardys headed off.

"We'll be back soon," Frank said.

When they were out of sight of the couple, Joe looked at his brother. "What do you think?"

"Of Ingrid? She seems nice enough. Not really Chet's type, though. I'd say she's more your speed."

Joe chuckled. "Before I started dating Vanessa, that is."

Frank smiled at his brother. "Right, *before,*" he said.

They turned left on the boardwalk and soon came to a partially completed longhouse. Only a few huge log timbers stood in place, and the structure loomed skeletonlike at the brink of the camp. Beyond it, a pristine pine forest stretched up the fog-shrouded hillside and into the distance.

"That must be the spot up ahead," Joe said. As he spoke, Joe glanced back toward his brother. Behind them, barely visible in the fog, he saw someone duck behind a building. Before Joe could mention it to Frank, though, they heard a sudden snap and a heavy groaning sound.

Frank spun around just in time to see the monstrous longhouse frame toppling toward them.

Chapter 2

"LOOK OUT!" FRANK YELLED.

He and Joe dived off the boardwalk as the heavy log framework clattered to the earth behind them, smashing into the spot where they had been standing seconds before.

"You okay?" Joe asked.

"I guess so. How about you?"

"I'm fine," Joe said, getting to his feet. "I wonder if that guy had something to do with this."

"What guy?"

"I saw a guy duck around a corner back there just before the frame fell on us."

"Let's see if we can catch him." Frank got to his feet and sprinted back the way they had come.

It took the brothers less than a minute to reach

the spot where Joe had seen the man. They rounded the corner at full tilt as two people came toward them. Joe stopped in time, but Frank crashed into a tall, well-built middle-aged man.

"Hey! What's going on here?" the man said. He stepped back and glared at the Hardys.

"Are you all right, Mr. Trudson?" asked the young man who had been walking beside him.

"Mr. Trudson? The head of Viking Village?" Joe said with a wince.

"Sorry about that, sir," Frank said. "I hope I didn't startle you."

"Of course not," Mr. Trudson said brusquely.

The last thing Frank wanted to do was get on Ivar Trudson's bad side. The owner of Viking Village stood well over six feet tall and was built like a weight lifter. His long blond hair hung past his shoulders, though it was very thin on the top of his head. Frank thought he looked powerful and menacing, like a modern-day Viking. Unlike his employees, however, he was dressed in jeans and a T-shirt with a Viking Village logo on it.

Mr. Trudson pushed past the Hardys and around the corner. From there he could clearly see the ruins of the longhouse. The big man leveled a stern look at Frank and Joe. "Are you responsible for this?"

"No, Mr. Trudson. We're not. Honest," Joe Hardy said in his most sincere voice.

"Who are you, anyway?" the owner asked.

"I'm Frank Hardy, and this is my brother,

Joe," said Frank. "We're friends of Chet Morton. You gave him permission to let us stay in his cabin." Frank extended his hand to shake.

Trudson ignored Frank's hand. "I may have made a mistake," he said, and walked toward the wreckage. "Chisholm," he said as he walked, "keep an eye on those two."

The young man turned to the Hardys. "I'm Dave Chisholm." He shook Joe's hand and then Frank's. "I work here."

"We guessed that from your clothes," Frank said, looking at Dave's Viking costume.

"He works here—sometimes," Trudson called back without slowing down. "I was just escorting him back to work after an 'extended' break."

Suddenly Chet appeared on the path leading from his cabin. Ingrid trailed just behind him. "What was that crash?" he asked as he came up to the three guys.

"I think there was a problem with the new building," Dave said.

The five of them walked to the longhouse, where Mr. Trudson was surveying the damage. Both Hardys heard the owner mutter quietly to himself, "We can't afford another delay."

Then he turned to the group and said in a normal tone of voice, "Well, there's no time for an investigation now. I'll have to check into what happened later."

He looked at Chet. "Morton, don't you have someplace to be?"

"Yes, Mr. Trudson. But I have something to report to you first."

"Well?"

"Somebody jumped me earlier when I was on my way to the parking lot."

Trudson frowned. "Do you know who it was? Were you hurt?"

"I didn't get a good look at him, but I'm fine," Chet said.

"Anything taken?" Mr. Trudson asked.

"No."

Trudson crossed his arms over his chest and shook his head. "Could this be someone's idea of a joke?" he asked, looking at the teens.

Frank spoke up. "If you're suggesting someone was just playing a trick on Chet, I don't think so. The attack looked pretty serious to us. I think you should call the police."

Mr. Trudson frowned. "At the Viking Village we like to take care of our problems in-house. I'll look into it."

"But—" Joe started.

"I *said* I'd look into it. Morton, I believe you have a job to do."

"Yes, sir," Chet said. "I'll get right to it, Mr. Trudson. Right after I change."

"Chisholm, Lampford, you're due for your shifts in the great hall. Let's go." Mr. Trudson headed toward the dining hall, and Dave and Ingrid followed.

Mr. Trudson turned back momentarily. "And

you Hardy boys—just try to stay out of everybody's way."

"We sure will," Joe said.

"Teenagers," they heard Trudson mutter as he, Ingrid, and Dave disappeared down the walkway.

"I feel sorry for you, having him for a boss," Frank said to Chet once Mr. Trudson was out of earshot.

"He's okay once you get used to him," Chet said. "Strict but fair." He started walking toward his cabin. "I have to change into my costume. I've got a battle to fight. You guys want to come with me?"

"I wouldn't miss it," Joe said.

It took only a few minutes for Chet to change, and Frank and Joe decided to wait outside the cabin.

When Chet stepped outside, Frank and Joe smiled. From the tip of his iron helmet to the toes of his fur-strapped boots Chet Morton looked every inch a Viking. He puffed out his chest, brandished an ax, and said loudly, "It's good to be a Viking."

"That looks sharp," Joe said. "Your ax, that is."

"It's just made to look that way," Chet said, leading the Hardys along with him. "It *is* metal, though. Could give you a nasty bump."

"So what's this battle you're fighting?" asked Frank.

"Just mock combat with one of the other staff members," Chet said.

"Like one of those medieval fairs?" Joe asked.

"I don't think Mr. Trudson will ever go that far," Chet said. "But he *has* been trying to make the place more commercial. Business hasn't been great."

"So, is this fight rehearsed?" Frank asked.

"Yeah. We practice a lot. I rehearse with five other guys, and we perform in rotation."

"Will you be the winner or the loser of this battle today?" Joe asked.

"I'm scheduled to lose today," Chet said. "But while you're here, I'm sure you'll get to see me win a fight or two."

Several minutes later they arrived at the demonstration square. It was a grassy area across from the Visitor Center, but the recent rain had turned it muddy. A few people had gathered on the nearby boardwalks, anticipating the event. The posted starting time was 5:45 P.M.

"Looks like we've got fifteen minutes," Joe said, checking his watch.

Chet fidgeted with his ax. "Yeah. But Mr. Trudson likes us to be early."

"Look, if you guys don't mind," Frank said, "I think I'll go and take a quick look at that longhouse. See if I can figure out why it nearly fell on us. I should make it back in time for the match."

"Don't worry about it," Chet said. "I'd rather you saw me *win* a match."

"Go ahead, Frank," Joe said. "Take your time.

I'll stay and catch the show. At least one of us should relax on this vacation."

Frank shook his head, then walked off.

"Is there a place to get some food around here?" Joe asked. "Maybe some popcorn or something?"

"Mr. Trudson doesn't believe in snack stands—the Vikings didn't have them—but the dining hall's just over there." Chet pointed past the Visitor Center to a huge longhouse, which Joe had noticed when they were on their way to Chet's cabin. "We could grab something quick before the match."

Though the hall didn't serve fast food, there were vending machines in the staff area. Chet and Joe gulped down some soda and chips before walking back across the yard.

"Sorry we had to eat so fast, Joe," Chet said. "But it's against policy to have any nontraditional foods in the exhibit areas."

"Don't worry, I like swallowing my tortilla chips whole."

By the time they got back, the crowd at the exhibit area had grown to several dozen people. The match was just minutes away, and Chet's opponent had arrived. He was a tall, bulky teenager with long black hair. He was wearing a huge horned helmet, and as he stalked around the square, he brandished a massive war hammer.

"Whoops," Chet muttered.

"What's wrong?" Joe asked.

"I forgot I was fighting Brandt Hill today."

"What difference does that make?"

"Well . . ." Chet said, "he doesn't really like me. He had his eye on Ingrid. I think he's jealous that I'm going out with her."

"Why didn't you mention this before? Jealousy is a pretty powerful motive," Joe said. "He could have been the guy who jumped you." Looking at Brandt Hill, Joe decided he was about the same size as the guy under the hooded gray cloak.

"Could be," Chet said. "But I don't think he's the kind of guy to choke somebody. If he did do it, I'm sure you and Frank will get the goods on him. Until then I can handle myself."

Joe clapped his friend on the back. "All right, Chet. Go get him. Knock him dead."

"I'd better not," Chet said, smiling. "I'm supposed to lose, remember?" He adjusted his costume and checked his weapon. Then he bellowed a huge war cry and stepped into the demonstration area.

Joe chuckled and stood back to watch the action.

The two opponents circled, appearing to size each other up. As they passed near him, Joe heard Brandt whisper, "Better do this the way we practiced, Morton, or you might get hurt."

Before Joe could decide if this was a real threat or just bravado, he was distracted by a voice from behind him. "This could never have happened," someone said quietly.

Obviously whoever it was didn't think much of the exhibition, Joe thought. He looked around to see who had spoken and saw a lanky red-haired man in his mid-twenties standing half a step behind him.

"Why couldn't it?" Joe asked, not fully turning away from the show.

"Well, for one thing," the man said, "their costumes are from two different periods. These guys never would have met. They should have shields, too. And the horns on that guy's helmet . . . There's no historical evidence that Viking helmets had horns. That's just something they made up in Hollywood."

"Hey, it's only a show," Joe said. "Why not just relax and enjoy it?" He walked away from the man to a spot where he could watch without commentary. The crowd was sparse enough that he found a place to himself.

The exhibition was heating up. The combatants had felt each other out with some preliminary moves, and now they were ready to attack.

Brandt roared and charged Chet, swinging his hammer as he came. Chet parried with his ax and ducked aside. Brandt recovered and swung at Chet's midsection. The Hardys' friend stepped back, narrowly avoiding the blow.

Joe smiled. Accurate or not, this was a good show, he thought. It must have taken a lot of rehearsal to put it together.

Chet stepped forward before his foe could recover and clubbed Brandt in the back with his free arm. Brandt staggered but ducked in time to avoid Chet's follow-up ax blow. He kicked back with one leg and just missed hitting Chet's left knee.

"Hey!" Chet exclaimed.

Joe noticed a look of surprise on Chet's face. "Hey!" wasn't a very Viking-like thing to say. Was Brandt Hill forgetting to stick to the script?

Brandt spun around and swung his hammer at Chet, hitting Chet's ax with great force. Before Chet could recover, Brandt charged forward and drove his shoulder into Chet's gut.

Chet let out a whoosh of air and stumbled backward, ending up not far from where Joe was standing. Because of the rain earlier that afternoon, the grass in the area was slick, and Chet almost lost his footing. He swung his ax wildly to keep Brandt at a safe distance. A look of panic flashed across Chet's face. "Stick to the script," he whispered to his opponent.

Brandt twirled his hammer. "What's the matter, Morton," he said under his breath, "you can't deal with a little improvisation?"

Joe looked around. Apparently none of the other spectators were close enough to hear the remark.

As Joe watched, beads of sweat formed on Chet's forehead, and he struggled to catch his breath. Brandt pressed his advantage, but Chet put up a strong defense. Suddenly, however, he hit a patch of wet earth. He fell to the ground on his back, and his helmet flew off.

The crowd gasped.

Joe knew there was no way the fall could have been scripted. Then he saw Brandt cock his arm and raise his hammer, aiming a deadly blow at Chet's head.

Chapter 3

JOE REARED BACK, took a flying leap, and hit Chet with one of his best football tackles, catching his friend in the ribs and shoving him out of the hammer's way.

The weapon splashed into the mud just inches from Joe's head.

The crowd gasped, then broke into wild applause. Brandt scowled and tossed his hammer into the dirt.

Chet and Joe, both covered with mud, quickly stood up. Chet was gasping for breath and glaring at his opponent. As the crowd dispersed, Joe thought he saw the red-haired man smile.

"What's the big idea of ruining the show?" Brandt Hill yelled at Joe.

"What are you talking about?" Joe responded

angrily. "Are you crazy? Chet slipped in the mud. You could have killed him."

"Morton knows enough to get out of the way," Brandt said. "We've rehearsed this a million times, and we always improvise. It's never a problem."

"Just as long as improvisation doesn't cave somebody's head in," Joe said. He wanted to punch this guy out but held himself back. He and Frank were already in enough trouble with the camp's owner.

"Trudson's going to hear about this," Brandt said. "And, Morton, you'd better stay out of my way." He scooped up his hammer and stalked off.

"Nice guy," Joe said under his breath.

"Yeah," Chet said.

Brandt spun around and pointed at Joe. "I heard that. You'd better keep out of my way, too." He turned and walked away again.

"Hey, thanks, Joe," Chet said. "I don't think I could have gotten out of the way in time. I kind of froze when I fell."

"You think Hill knew that?"

"I don't know." Chet bent down and retrieved his helmet. "He could have. The fall wasn't really his fault, though. I should have been more careful."

"He's the one who should have been more careful, if you ask me."

"Hey, you guys look great." It was Frank, back from investigating the longhouse collapse. "What did I miss? Did you decide to take up mud wrestling?"

"We'll tell you about it on the way to the cabin," Chet said. "I need to shower and change before my evening shift. Mr. Trudson will kill me if I show up looking like this."

"Did you find anything at the longhouse?" Joe asked Frank as they walked.

"Somebody sawed through one of the main support beams," Frank said. "Just the right one to bring the whole frame down. No way the collapse could have been accidental. The tooth marks looked as if they were made by a pretty small saw."

"You won't find any modern saws around here," Chet said. "Mr. Trudson only allows us to use period tools. Vikings didn't have little bitty saws."

"That would be wimpy," Frank said.

"Right," Chet said. "Usually we just break trees in half with our bare hands."

Frank and Joe both laughed.

"Construction must be pretty time-consuming and expensive, using only period tools," Joe said.

"It sure takes a while, and I guess it must cost more. But Mr. Trudson's a nut for historical accuracy."

"Anyway," Frank continued, "there's no way to tell if someone meant that building to hit us or if we were just in the wrong place at the wrong time. Either way, it looks as if somebody's sabotaging the place."

Chet and Joe filled Frank in on the fight as they showered, changed, then rinsed off their clothing. They hung their wet clothing out to dry on a line beside Chet's cabin.

"Hope this doesn't shrink," Joe said, hanging up his red letter jacket.

"It's seen worse," Frank said. "I don't think a little mud is going to wreck it."

"Yeah. If I didn't know better, I'd think that jacket was made out of Kevlar," Chet said.

Joe caught a glimpse of a chain around his friend's neck. "Hey, Chet," he said. "Do I see you're wearing jewelry now? Is that some kind of a Viking thing?"

"No . . . and yes," Chet said. He pulled the chain out from under his shirt. On it was a silver ring with a cross design engraved on it. "I don't think the Vikings wore chains around their necks, but the ring has a Viking design on it," Chet said, displaying it for the Hardys to see.

"A token from Ingrid?" Frank asked.

"Nah. It's the ring I found. I told you about it in my letter. Remember? Anyway, I asked around, but it didn't seem to belong to anybody, so I kept it. I thought it was my good-luck charm—until today."

"Who knows?" Joe said. "Without it, you might be dead."

Chet smiled. "Yeah. Twice. Guess I should

hang on to it then, eh? At least until you catch the guy who attacked me." Frank could tell that even though Chet was trying to make light of the attacks, he was actually pretty concerned.

"What time is it?" Chet asked.

Frank checked his watch. "Six-thirty."

"We'd better get going or I won't have time to eat dinner before my evening shift."

They filed out of Chet's cabin and hiked off toward the dining hall.

When they got to the great hall, they entered through the guest entrance. "Shouldn't you be going through the employees' entrance?" Frank asked.

"Mr. Trudson's policy is to have the costumed staff eat with the guests," Chet said. "He says it gives the customers a better feel for the period and gives them a chance to ask questions."

Frank looked around the long, high-ceilinged room. He noted that the walls were constructed of stone, with huge timbers supporting the thatched roof. There were low benches along the walls with rough wooden tables set in front of them. A huge fire in the middle of the room, along with the torches that lined the walls, provided the only lighting. Smoke from the fire wafted out through a big hole in the ceiling. It was a very convincing Viking atmosphere, he thought.

Frank and Joe paid for their meals at the door,

and Chet signed in on the staff list as they entered.

Guests and staff filled the room with a great din of activity. Serving men and women bustled about the room carrying wooden trenchers, large boards piled with bowls of food. A young woman in a long dress spotted Chet and waved him and the Hardys over to her table. Chet smiled back and headed in her direction. In his hurry he almost collided with one of his fellow workers.

"Sorry, Scott," Chet said to the guy he'd almost bumped into.

"No problem. Heads up, though." Scott smiled at Chet. "Got to get back to work. No rest for the weary Viking." He headed out the door.

"Who was that?" Frank asked.

"Scott Thompkins. He's an okay guy, especially considering he's Brandt Hill's roommate," Chet said. "Much more easygoing."

"He'd have to be," Joe said.

When they reached the table, the young woman stood to greet them. She was pretty, with curly, dark blond hair and hazel eyes. "Hey, Chet, how's it going? Who're these hunks?" she asked.

"Hi, Claire. It's going okay. These movie stars are my friends Frank and Joe Hardy. They're visiting me for a few days, so treat them right. Guys, Claire Benson. She rooms with Ingrid."

Claire smiled and shook hands with the Hardys. "Pleased to meet you," she said. "I just got here. Care to join me for dinner?"

"Don't mind if we do," Joe said, pulling the table out a bit so he could slide in and sit down. Frank and Chet did the same.

The hall was arranged so that all the tables faced the center of the room and the diners sat with their backs to the wall. Servers passed from table to table with huge trays of food.

Joe looked at the wooden spoon and fork he'd been given. "Primitive," he said, "very primitive." Then he noticed someone across the room. "Hey, Frank, see that redheaded guy standing over there in the Viking outfit?"

Frank looked in the direction his brother was looking. "Yeah."

"He was at Chet's fight complaining about the lack of historical accuracy. I thought he was a guest, but now he's wearing a costume."

"That's Hank Walsh," Claire said. "He works here, too. He's a real pain in the neck, though. Even more of a stickler for history than Ivar Trudson—if that's possible."

"The fight wasn't authentic enough for him," Joe said.

"He's not too keen on this eating hall, either," Claire said.

Frank looked around, trying to see what might bother a history buff. "I just noticed, the torches are electric, aren't they?"

"Yes," Claire said. "Mr. Trudson wanted to use real ones, but the fire marshal wouldn't allow it. Made him put in a modern kitchen, too. This floor's not dirt, either, just cast concrete made to look like earth."

"I noticed that as soon as I stepped on it," Joe said.

"And if you look carefully," she continued, "you can see a sprinkler system and emergency lights tucked up near the roof. There's lots of little stuff like that throughout the attraction. The only people really bugged by it are Mr. Trudson and Hank Walsh, although the two of them don't see eye to eye on what's historically accurate either."

"I guess sometimes realism has to take a back-seat to safety," Joe said.

Frank studied Hank Walsh, who was bussing tables unenthusiastically. "He's kind of old for this job, isn't he?" Frank asked.

"I guess so," Claire said. "But this place is usually hiring, and you know how the economy is. Anything that'll put food on the table."

"Speaking of food," Chet said, "I need to get some in my stomach." He stood up. "Hey, Dave." He motioned to Dave Chisholm, who was serving another table.

"Be with you in a minute," Dave replied. Joe noticed that Brandt Hill was sitting at the table Dave Chisholm had just served. Joe indicated the table to his brother. "That's him," he whispered. "Brandt Hill."

Frank looked at Hill who, having noticed Chet, was scowling in their direction. "Probably best to stay out of his way," Frank whispered to his brother.

"Sure . . . as long as he stays out of ours," Joe said.

Chet snagged Dave Chisholm as he walked past them with another tray of food.

"Whoa," Dave said as Chet scooped the tray out of his hands. "What are you doing?"

"Don't worry, Dave," Chet said, smiling. "There's plenty more where that came from."

"We're growing boys, you know," Joe added.

Dave frowned at them and stalked off to get another tray.

"Here we go," Chet said, setting the tray in front of his friends. "Thought I'd better take things into my own hands." He smiled. "Sometimes the service here is terrible."

"That's 'cause they hire slackers like you, Chet," Claire said.

"I don't see *you* working, Claire," Chet replied, grinning.

Frank and Joe both chuckled.

The tray Chet had appropriated was filled with breads, soups, vegetables, and meats as well as several dishes the Hardys couldn't identify.

After serving his friends, Chet picked up a bowl of food and put it to his lips.

"What is this?" Joe asked, poking the jellylike white mass with his fork.

"Lutefisk," Claire said. "Jellied codfish. Try it. It's really tasty."

Joe made a face. "It's a wonder the Vikings had any energy after eating this stuff," Joe said. He decided to stick to food that he knew would be edible.

"They probably had indigestion, which is what gave them their nasty edge," Frank said.

"The lutefisk's okay," Chet said, "but I like this codfish pudding better." He lifted another bowl to his lips and made a loud slurping sound.

"Isn't that bad manners?" Frank asked.

Chet put the bowl down just enough to answer. "Nah. It's authentic. Plus it makes a good show for the guests."

"Does Chet eat this way at home?" Claire asked the Hardys. "Looks like he's had a lot of practice."

The Hardys chuckled, and so did Chet, but suddenly his laughter turned to gasps. He dropped his half-full bowl and staggered to his feet, clutching his throat.

Chapter 4

CLAIRE STOOD UP and said, "Somebody do something. He's choking!"

Still clutching his throat, Chet bumped into the table and toppled it. Food splattered everywhere as plates clattered onto the concrete floor.

Frank and Joe leaped from their seats simultaneously. Frank got a grip on Chet from behind, clenched his arms around his stomach, and squeezed hard. Pop! Something shot out of Chet's mouth and landed on the floor.

Chet took deep breaths of air. "It's okay. I'm all right," he gasped. A small crowd was gathering around him. "No problem, folks," he said. "You can all go back to dinner."

Several other staff members came over to right the table and wipe up the floor. Joe scooped up the offending object as Frank and Claire helped Chet back to his seat. "Thanks, Frank," Chet wheezed. "Guess I owe both you and Joe today."

"Forget it," Frank said. "Just don't eat so fast, and it won't happen again."

"Look at that creep Brandt," Joe said. "He's smiling. I'd like to punch his lights out."

Ingrid pushed her way through the crowd to Chet. Brandt's smile turned to a scowl when he saw her.

"Chet, are you all right? What happened?" she asked.

"I just choked on some food," Chet said, looking embarrassed.

"This isn't food; it's a stone," Joe said, turning the object over in his hand.

"Well, that's weird," Claire said.

"Stone soup isn't another Viking tradition, is it?" Frank asked.

"Not that I know of," Ingrid said. She held out a hand to Joe. "Why don't you let me toss it out when I get back to the kitchen?"

Joe closed his hand around the object. "Nah. I think I'll hang on to this for a while."

Just then Ivar Trudson strode over to Chet. "You okay, Morton?" he asked. Chet nodded.

The village owner clapped him on the shoulder, then turned to the rest of the hall. "Sorry for the interruption, folks. Everything's okay now. You can go back to enjoying your meal."

The servers ushered all the guests back to their tables, but Mr. Trudson lingered behind.

"Lampford," he said, "back to the kitchen."

"Yes, sir," Ingrid said, curtsying and hurrying off.

"Morton," Mr. Trudson said, "take the rest of the night off. I heard about your trouble with Hill. Three accidents in one day is too much. I don't know what's going on, but I want you out of circulation until things settle down."

"But—" Chet began, then thought better of whatever he had been about to say. "Yes, sir."

"Just make sure you're one hundred percent ready for work tomorrow," Mr. Trudson said. He turned and mingled with the patrons for a while, making small talk. Joe noticed that he stopped talking when he saw an attractive woman in a navy blue suit. When their eyes met, he stared at her briefly. Then, without a word, he turned and abruptly left the hall.

Joe wondered what that was all about. It wasn't an obviously hostile glance, but Mr. Trudson clearly seemed surprised to see the woman.

"I don't know about the rest of you," Chet said, "but I've kind of lost my appetite."

"Gee, what a surprise," Joe said, "considering you almost swallowed this." He opened his hand, held out the stone, and noticed for the first time that something had been carved on it. Looking closer, he saw it was a crude image of a human being. "Hey," he said, "check this out." Frank,

Chet, and Claire all leaned over to have a closer look.

Frank frowned as he looked at the image on the stone. "Do you think it's American Indian?"

"Might be Viking," Claire replied. "But I'm no expert. Maybe you could have Mr. Trudson check it out later."

"Whatever it is, I don't want to find any more of them in my food," Chet said.

Joe put the stone in his jeans pocket. "I think I'll save it," he said. "It could be an ancient Viking choking stone."

"One of their more effective models," Chet said.

"Okay, I've had enough excitement for one meal," Claire said. "Time to get back to work." She stood up and straightened her costume. "I'm doing a demonstration on hand weaving. You can't see the patterns so well once it gets dark. Those oil lamps don't give off a lot of light, you know." She gave the others a wave and left the hall.

"What do you say we take a little tour of the place?" Frank said.

"Good idea," Joe said. "We can always pick up a snack later."

"I could use some air," Chet said. "Follow me." He and the Hardys got up and headed for the door. Frank noticed that Brandt Hill followed them with his eyes as they left the building.

"Mr. Trudson seemed a lot more concerned with keeping the customers happy than with you almost choking to death, Chet," Frank said once they were outside.

"I noticed that, too," Joe said.

"He has been acting sort of strange lately," Chet said.

"How do you mean?" Frank asked.

"Well, he's always been pretty serious, but for the past couple of weeks he's really been in a bad mood. He comes down hard on anybody who's slacking off, and he's gotten even more obsessed with historical accuracy."

"You mean he's been taking heat for that," Joe said. "That Walsh character seemed pretty prickly."

"Walsh is pretty open about his criticism—except when Mr. Trudson's around. He's careful not to mouth off in front of the boss. I think Mr. Trudson would boot him out pretty quickly if he ever heard him cutting the place down. Trudson's very touchy about the subject. He took some flak from the media when he opened the place, I guess."

"What do you mean?" Frank asked as they passed an unfinished long hall and turned toward the woods near the guest parking lot.

"Trudson founded the village after discovering a rune stone on the property about four years ago," Chet began.

"Rune stone?" Joe asked.

"Right. Runes are ancient characters, like the letters of our alphabet, that the Vikings carved on wood and stone. The Vikings supposedly passed through here in the thirteen hundreds and inscribed on this stone the story of their journey. From what I understand, there was a lot of argument about whether the stone was real or not. Some people say it's a fake."

"Are you saying people would actually fake history to make a buck?" Joe asked in mock horror.

Chet chuckled and continued, "Mr. Trudson built this whole attraction around the stone. He's convinced it's authentic, and he gets pretty steamed when anyone says otherwise."

Frank wasn't concerned about history at the moment. "Let's check out the woods," he suggested. "Maybe we can find some tracks from that guy who jumped you."

As they headed for the spot where the attack had taken place, Frank scanned the ground carefully.

"Mr. Trudson must have a lot of money tied up in this place," Joe said.

"I guess," Chet said. "I know he doesn't have a lot of time for anything else. He hardly ever goes home. He has a small cabin on the east side of the property, but I've never seen him use it. Mostly he stays in his office."

"Doesn't he have a family? Wife? Kids?"

"Nope," Chet said. "I once heard him mention a brother, but that's it. His whole life revolves around Viking Village."

"So where's the rune stone?" Frank asked.

"Mr. Trudson keeps it locked up in a big glass case in the Visitor Center," Chet said. "He doesn't let anyone examine it up close anymore."

"Sounds suspicious," Joe said. "Maybe he knows it's a fake."

"Maybe," Chet said. "Mostly I think he's just tired of all the controversy." He picked up a pinecone and tossed it into the woods. "I know *I* would be if I were him. I'm exhausted after what's happened."

"I don't blame you," Joe said, grinning. "A boy of your delicate constitution." Chet gave him a playful punch.

They had reached the place where Chet was attacked. Frank studied the area. It was easy to see how someone could disappear in the thick stands of trees, he thought. As he looked around, he caught a quick flash of movement out of the corner of his eye. "Look out!" Frank yelled as they heard a loud crack, then a whooshing sound coming from above.

Chapter 5

FRANK SHOVED JOE AND CHET out of the way just as a tall pine tree came crashing down toward them. All three teenagers fell sprawling to the ground as the topmost branches bounced to a halt on top of them. It was getting dark, and Frank hadn't spotted the threat until it was almost too late.

"Sorry about that," Frank said as they scrambled to their feet.

"No problem," Joe said.

"Look over there!" Chet shouted. The Hardys followed his outstretched hand and saw a large man darting off through the woods—a man dressed not just in a cloak but in full Viking costume.

"After him!" In an instant Joe was sprinting toward the Viking with Frank right behind.

"I'll wait here in case he doubles back," Chet yelled after them, picking up a broken branch and brandishing it like a club.

The evening shadows made it difficult for the Hardys to see their quarry. The man obviously knew these woods, Frank thought, because he zigzagged between trees and ducked low-hanging branches with ease.

"He runs pretty well for a ghost," Joe said.

"Do you recognize him?" Frank asked.

"No. But I didn't get a good look."

After a few minutes the Hardys broke out of the woods at the edge of a narrow, swift-running river.

"Which way did he go?" Joe said.

"Beats me," Frank said. There was no sign of the Viking anywhere; upstream he could hear a waterfall, but he couldn't detect any human sounds.

"Let's head back to Chet," Joe said. "Maybe we can pick up some kind of clue on the way."

"Seems like that guy just ran us around in circles," Joe said as they headed back the way they'd come.

"I think Chet's just—" Suddenly Frank spotted a flash of clothing in the bushes. Without another word he darted into the bracken to his right. He found a man crouched there, grabbed him by the collar, and pulled him out. Something fell from the man's hand as Frank collared him. Frank cocked his fist back, ready to slam it into the intruder's face. Then he realized the man wasn't in costume. "You're not a Viking," he said.

"Are you crazy?" The man shook himself free of Frank's grip. He was tall and wiry, with dark hair. He wore camouflage clothing and a hat, and a pair of binoculars hung from a leather strap around his neck. Frank saw that the object he'd dropped was an unlit propane lantern.

"Who are you? What are you doing here?" Joe asked.

"I'm Nick Osgood, and I'm a bird-watcher," he said.

"You're bird-watching?" Frank said. "At night? On private property?"

"I'm looking for northern spotted owls. And if this is private property, it's news to me."

"Have you seen any Vikings?" Joe asked.

Osgood looked at him. "No. I haven't seen any pirates, either."

"Let's go, Joe," Frank said with disgust. "Chet's probably wondering what happened to us."

"You probably ought to get out of here, mister," Joe said, "before folks from Viking Village figure out you're trespassing."

"Whatever you say, kid," Mr. Osgood said, picking up his lantern as Frank and Joe walked away.

The Hardys quickly found Chet, who was standing by a tree stump, branch in hand.

"Still guarding the area?" Joe asked.

"Right, Joe. I know how upset you get if you don't have a place to park yourself." He nodded toward the tree stump. "I guess you didn't catch the Viking."

"Nope, he got away," Joe said. "But we did collar a nervous bird-watcher."

Frank bent to examine the stump of the fallen tree. "Looks like someone cut this down with an ax. Pretty expertly, I'd say."

"Whoever it was probably chopped almost all the way through it, then waited till we came around and shoved it over on us," Joe said. "Another ambush."

"A lot of the village folk are good with axes," Chet said.

"Including Brandt Hill?" Joe said.

"Yeah. I guess. Among others. Like I said, we take shifts working on the new construction."

Frank nodded. "Well, it's getting too dark to do any more investigating. Let's head back. We can look for tracks in the morning."

The three of them headed toward the village, and soon they were on the familiar log walks.

"Could we pick up something from the dining hall?" Joe asked. "I'm still pretty hungry."

"Sounds good to me," Chet agreed.

The great hall was almost empty when they arrived, but one of the kitchen staff put together a platter of leftovers.

After they had eaten, Chet said, "I'll take you back to my cabin by the scenic route." He turned left at a half-finished guesthouse and headed toward the earthen wall that separated the village from the staff areas.

Frank paused as they passed a small building. He could hear loud voices inside. "Hey, isn't that Mr. Trudson?"

"Yep," Chet said. "That's his office."

"Do you know who he's arguing with?" Joe asked.

Chet shrugged. "Sounds like a woman," he said, "but I don't recognize her voice."

All three teens stood still for a moment, but they couldn't make out what was being said. As they listened, the door to the office opened, and a woman came out.

"We'll be discussing this again, Ivar," she said, "when you're a little calmer and more rational." She brushed past the teens without acknowledging them and headed down the log walk, her heels clacking on the wood. It was the woman they'd seen earlier in the dining hall.

"Do you recognize her?" Joe asked.

"Ronalda Pearl," Chet said. "She's a local businesswoman. Real estate, I think."

"Mr. Trudson didn't seem too happy to see her in the dining hall. Any idea why?"

"Nope," Chet said, looking around somewhat nervously. "Let's go. I wouldn't want Trudson to catch us hanging around."

They walked past the office, through an opening in the berm, and into another area filled with staff cabins.

"Where are we going?" Joe asked.

"I want to show you the rec room," Chet said. "There's a phone inside, in case you ever need it. There are also some vending machines if you ever get the munchies after the dining hall has closed."

"A vital fact," Joe said, smiling.

"I'll show you how to get into the staff parking area, too, so you can move the van out of the visitors' lot," Chet said.

"Good idea," Frank agreed.

"Hey, Morton, is that you?" someone asked behind them.

All three teens turned to see Scott Thompkins walking in their direction. "I thought I heard your voice, Morton. I think you may have something of mine. Claire mentioned you found a carved stone in your food. Somebody boosted one from my cabin earlier today, so I'd like to take a look at it."

Joe pulled the stone out of his pocket. "Is this it?"

Scott took the stone from Joe and examined it. "Yep. That's mine, all right." He turned to Chet. "How'd it get in your food?"

"Beats me," Chet said. "Maybe someone thought it'd give the codfish some extra flavor."

Scott chuckled. "Well, thanks." He stuck the artifact in his pocket and headed for his cabin.

Joe watched as Scott walked the few yards to his hut, opened the door, and went inside.

Frank turned to Joe. "What did you do *that* for?" he asked.

"What did he do?" Chet asked.

"He gave away our evidence," Frank said.

"I didn't exactly have a choice," Joe said.

"I know you guys think someone's out to get me," said Chet, "but there's just no way it was Scott."

"Didn't you tell us that Scott Thompkins is Brandt Hill's roommate?" Joe asked. "It would have been pretty easy for Hill to take that stone and drop it in your food."

"He's right, Chet," Frank said. "Dave Chisholm served Brandt's table right before ours."

"Along with every other table in our section," said Chet. "And he didn't expect me to take the tray from him," he added. "Anyway, don't worry about me. I can handle my problems with Brandt Hill. You guys concentrate on catching that Viking."

"Well," Joe said, "we know who the stone belongs to. I guess that's about it for now."

After touring the rec room, checking out the vending machines, and moving the van to the staff parking lot, they went back to Chet's cabin. Chet and Joe fell quickly asleep, but Frank stayed awake for a while. His mind whirled with possibilities.

Who had put the stone in Chet's food? Was

it definitely Brandt Hill? No way was it Dave Thompkins; he wouldn't have tipped his hand by asking Joe to give it back. Were the attacks on Chet part of the sabotage, or were they separate incidents?

And what about the Viking that Ingrid and Chet had talked about? Was he the same guy who had jumped Chet? Frank wished they'd gotten a clearer look at him. Maybe the weather would be better tomorrow. They might find some tracks or other clues.

Still trying to put the pieces together, Frank drifted off into an uneasy sleep.

"Oh, man, look at my coat!" Joe moaned.

Morning had not brought better weather. It was foggy, there was a steady drizzle, and Joe's letter jacket was dripping wet. Frank knew the rain had probably obliterated any footprints they might have found.

"Don't worry, Joe," Chet said. "I have an extra jacket and a baseball cap that I can loan you. I've got to work today, and I was hoping you guys would get to see the village the way it would have been hundreds of years ago. But with this rain . . ."

"I think this *is* the way it was hundreds of years ago," Frank said as he threw on a corduroy jacket and pulled up the collar.

"Yeah, you're probably right," Chet said.

Chet handed Joe a baseball cap and a brightly

colored nylon jacket, then put on his Viking cloak. Joe donned his borrowed gear, and they stepped out into the rain.

They went to the great hall and ate breakfast. Then Chet gave the Hardys another quick tour, hitting some spots they'd missed the night before. They started at the small farm at the northeast end of the village, walked through the town, and then stopped briefly at the Visitor Center.

Frank and Joe caught just a brief glimpse of the rune stone, however, before Ivar Trudson walked in with Ronalda Pearl on his heels. Rather than interfere in Trudson's discussion, the teens decided to leave him alone. They could ask about the mugging and perhaps examine the rune stone later.

"You know," Joe said as they left the building, "maybe we should find Scott Thompkins and ask him a few questions."

"I was thinking the same thing," Frank said. "I saw him working at the farm when we passed by."

"Well, I have to get to work." Chet flexed his muscles. "I'm smithing in the forge today."

"I guess that makes you Iron Man Morton for the day," Frank said.

"Yeah," replied Chet. "You should see the girls fall over when I flex my pecs."

"Maybe that's because you forgot to put on some deodorant," Joe said.

Chet waved his friends off. "Scram! Out of here. Get lost in the rain."

"Don't take any wooden horseshoes," Joe called after Chet as he walked off toward the forge.

It took the brothers only a few minutes to walk back to the farm.

"I haven't seen Scott since he went on his break," said a man in a green tunic whom the Hardys found working there. "He was supposed to be back half an hour ago. If you see him tell him to get over here before Mr. Trudson figures out he's slacking off."

"Don't worry, we will," Frank said.

"Let's check his cabin." Joe said.

They bumped into Claire on her way out of the weavers' hut. She was dressed in a heavy maroon cloak and long red dress and was carrying a basket.

"Hey, Claire," Frank said.

"Hi, Frank . . . Is that you, Joe? I almost thought you were Chet."

"My jacket got messed up," Joe said. "Chet lent me his and the cap."

"The baseball cap looks good on you," Claire said, smiling.

"Have you seen Scott Thompkins anywhere?" Frank asked.

"No, I haven't. If he's not working, he should be in his cabin."

"That's where we're headed," Joe said. Then, looking at the basket, he asked, "How about you?"

"If you can believe it, I'm going into the woods to pick wild raspberries."

"The way you were dressed I thought you might be going to Grandma's house," Joe said.

Claire paused. "Oh, right. Little Red Riding Hood." She smiled. "Well, I'll see you wolves later."

Frank and Joe waved as she strolled down the boardwalk toward the woods. Joe resisted the urge to cut loose with a wolf whistle.

"I'm thirsty," Joe said. "Where's the nearest soda machine?"

"The rec room," Frank said. "I'll meet you there. I need to get my rain jacket out of the van."

"Okay."

Frank jogged off toward the parking lot and quickly disappeared into the fog. Joe headed for the staff area.

It was silent in the village. Apparently the rainy weather was keeping guests away and driving the staff indoors, Joe thought. He imagined how life must have been for real Vikings living in such a place. They probably felt very much as he did now.

Joe smiled as he passed through the berm. The wall gave him a sense of security; it protected the town from its enemies.

Just as he was entertaining that thought, somebody hit him hard from behind.

Chapter 6

JOE STAGGERED under the impact of the blow but managed to stay on his feet. He tried to spin around, but the attacker quickly pinned his arms to his sides.

The guy was strong, Joe thought, whoever he was. Maybe he was the same one who had jumped Chet the day before.

Joe ducked forward and twisted to his right in a quick judo move. The attacker lost his footing, and Joe slipped free, but as he turned to face his foe, the guy landed a haymaker on Joe's jaw.

Joe staggered backward, partly from the blow and partly from surprise that the guy throwing the punch was Brandt Hill. A look of pure hatred danced in Brandt's eyes. "Trying to steal my girlfriend, huh?" he said. Brandt stepped forward, aiming another punch at Joe's head.

Fighting off the stars in front of his eyes, Joe sidestepped Hill's follow-up blow and lashed out with his foot, catching the black-haired teen in the thigh.

Brandt grunted and staggered sideways. For the first time he got a good look at Joe's face. "Hey, you're not Morton!" he exclaimed.

"You got that right," Joe said. Maybe wearing Chet's jacket and baseball cap hadn't been such a good idea after all, he thought as he aimed a right cross at Brandt's jaw.

Hill ducked, and Joe caught him on the side of the head, the force of the blow stunning Brandt for a moment. Joe followed up with a left to Brandt's midsection, but he deflected it and jammed his elbow into Joe's chin.

Joe grunted as his teeth clacked together. Then he jerked his head forward, butting Brandt in the temple. Brandt blinked and took a step back.

Joe closed in, aimed a punch at his opponent's gut, and connected, doubling him over. But Brandt lunged forward, driving his shoulder into Joe's stomach. Joe spun like a matador stepping away from a charging bull. He could taste blood in his mouth.

Brandt turned, and the two faced each other across a short distance. Staff members who were working in the vicinity gathered together, watching and talking among themselves.

"Joe!" Frank called as he raced in from the parking lot. Then Chet came jogging from the nearby forge.

"So," Brandt said, "you need two other guys to take me on, Morton? Come on, I'm ready!"

"What's your problem?" Chet asked.

Brandt scowled at him. "Nothing that your leaving town wouldn't solve. I'm tired of you making plays for my girlfriend."

"Ingrid's not your girlfriend," Chet said, his face reddening with anger.

"You're pretty brave with your friends around, Morton."

"And *you're* pretty brave, jumping people from behind," Joe said. He wanted to charge Brandt again, but Frank held him back.

"You jumped me from behind yesterday," Chet said to Brandt. "Now you did the same thing to Joe. What's the matter? Are you afraid to fight face-to-face?"

"You're crazy, Morton. I never laid a hand on you," Brandt said. "I *still* haven't. You probably got your buddy there to dress up like you just 'cause you're too chicken to face me."

Chet's eyes narrowed, and he took a step forward. Brandt clenched his fists, ready to fight.

"All right, break it up." The commanding voice belonged to Ivar Trudson. With his arrival, both Chet and Brandt backed off.

Joe looked around. A crowd of staff members had gathered. Joe spotted Dave Chisholm and

Hank Walsh, but he didn't see Scott Thompkins. Dave and Hank slipped off quickly as soon as the fight was over. Joe noted they were both careful not to attract Ivar Trudson's attention.

"I don't know what's going on between you two," Mr. Trudson said to Chet and Brandt, "but this is the end of it. I won't tolerate brawling in this village." He looked sternly at both boys. "This is your last warning. If I catch either of you at something like this again, you're out of here. Understand?"

"Yes, Mr. Trudson," Chet said.

"Yes, sir," Brandt said, but he shot a look at Chet that told Frank and Joe this wasn't over.

"Both of you, back to your cabins for the rest of the day," Trudson said. "Either you come out ready to *work* tomorrow morning or you pack your things and head home." He looked directly at Brandt Hill. "And if you see that roommate of yours, tell him he has one hour to get back to his post or he's fired."

Mr. Trudson turned and started toward his office. "The rest of you, back to work. As if I don't have enough to worry about . . ."

The crowd dispersed quickly.

Brandt turned and headed toward the staff parking lot.

"Hey," Chet said, "Mr. Trudson told you to go back to your cabin."

"Mind your own business," Brandt said. "And stop trying to act so tough."

"I'm tough enough to take *you* out."

Brandt turned back toward him. "Prove it."

"Any time. You just name the place."

Brandt turned away again. "Forget it. You aren't worth losing this crummy job over. Not today, anyway." He stalked off. "I'm going to take a ride and get away from the stench of this place."

"I hope Trudson cans you for it," Chet called after him. He turned to his friends. "I'm going back to my hut. I've got some reading to catch up on, anyway."

"Want us to come with you?" Frank asked.

"No, thanks. I'd just bore you guys to death. Besides, I know you want to poke around some more. I'm counting on you to find the saboteur." Chet smiled, then turned and walked off toward his cabin. "Bring me a soda later, if you don't mind."

"Sure thing," Joe said. "Let's go check Brandt and Dave's cabin."

He and Frank headed in that direction. "Do you think Brandt was telling the truth about not jumping Chet?" Joe asked as they walked.

Frank frowned. "It's hard to say," he said. "He didn't mind going toe-to-toe."

"On the other hand, he did jump me from behind," Joe said.

"Maybe that's how he likes to get started," Frank said.

As they approached the cabin Scott Thompkins

shared with Brandt Hill, the Hardys noticed that the door was ajar.

"That's strange," Frank said quietly.

"Maybe Brandt left the door open," Joe said, "or maybe Scott's inside."

"There's only one way to find out." Frank pushed the door open all the way. "Anybody home?" he called. "Scott? It's Frank and Joe Hardy, Chet's friends."

There was no answer. The brothers poked their heads inside.

"Nobody here," Frank said.

"And it doesn't look as if anything's been disturbed," Joe said. "What next?"

Before Frank could answer, a distant scream shattered the stillness.

Frank and Joe immediately took off in the direction of the scream, slamming the cabin door behind them.

"I think it came from the woods," Joe said, leading the way.

They heard the scream again. A few other staff members followed the Hardys, but Frank and Joe's athletic prowess kept them well ahead. They left the boardwalk and headed uphill into the woods at full speed. They heard another scream.

"This sounds serious," Joe said. They kept following the sound, and soon they burst into a clearing by the river.

Claire was kneeling there, tears streaming

down her face, her basket overturned and raspberries spilled everywhere. She didn't seem to be hurt, Joe noticed. Why was she screaming like that?

Then Frank and Joe saw what she was looking at.

Nearby, at the foot of an ancient pine, lay Scott Thompkins, unconscious, his left arm deeply gashed and blood gushing everywhere.

Chapter 7

FRANK AND JOE raced to Scott's side.

"Claire, give me your cloak," Frank said. Claire stood and silently handed the cloak to Frank. He quickly tore it into strips, then took one of them and pressed it to Scott's wound.

Joe grabbed Claire by both shoulders, looked her in the eye, and spoke calmly. "We need you to get an ambulance—fast."

Claire nodded, took a deep breath, and raced back toward the village.

The next twenty-five minutes went slowly for the Hardys. Fortunately, their first-aid training allowed them to keep Scott alive until the paramedics arrived. They managed to stop the bleeding by tying one strip of the cloak tightly around Scott's upper arm as a tourniquet and pressing the others over the wound.

Since the regular ambulance couldn't handle the terrain, the hospital had had to requisition a four-wheel-drive vehicle from the fire department, which took more time. Once the paramedics arrived, however, they reacted quickly. Almost everyone in the village gathered around as the paramedics put Scott on a stretcher, slid the stretcher into the makeshift ambulance, then slammed the doors shut. Moments later the vehicle sped off, sirens wailing.

The police had arrived just after the ambulance. They wasted no time clearing the area around the crime scene and surrounding it with yellow tape. The cops quickly began conducting preliminary interviews.

Frank and Joe took a few minutes to clean themselves up in the river. Just as they were returning to the scene of the crime, Chet Morton jogged casually up the hill to where they were standing. He was dressed in a gray running suit. A pair of headphones hung around his neck.

"What's going on?" he asked.

"Chet, where have you been? Mars?" Joe asked.

"I was just reading. Plus I had my headphones on full blast. I didn't know anything was going on until I saw people running up through the woods."

"Scott Thompkins nearly bled to death. Somebody whacked him in the arm, probably with an ax. The injury looks pretty bad," Frank said.

Chet's face went pale. "Oh, man."

A young police officer walked over to the three teens. "Are you Frank and Joe Hardy?" he asked.

"Yes, sir." It seemed strange to Joe to call the police officer "sir." The guy didn't look much older than he and Frank.

"I heard you saved the boy's life," the policeman said. "I'm Officer Mark Haddad of the Burton Police Department. I'd like to ask you a few questions."

"Sure," the Hardys said at the same time.

"What about me?" asked Chet.

"Just leave your name with the lead officer and go back to whatever you were doing. We'd really like to keep people out of this area."

Chet walked over to the officer who seemed to be coordinating the scene, had a few words with him, and then headed back toward his cabin.

"You guys were on the scene pretty early. Did you see anything?" Officer Haddad asked Frank and Joe.

"No," said Joe. "We got here after Claire Benson. By the time we arrived, the perpetrator was already gone."

"Did Claire see who did it?" Frank asked.

"No. He was already—" Officer Haddad began, then stopped. "Hold on. Who's supposed to be asking the questions here?" He leveled a serious look at the Hardys.

"Sorry," Frank said. "We're used to asking

questions. Our dad, Fenton Hardy, is a P.I., and we've worked with him on a lot of cases."

Officer Haddad raised an eyebrow at the mention of Mr. Hardy's name. "Okay, so you guys are some kind of amateur detectives and your father's a famous P.I. But no matter who you are, this is still an official police investigation, so leave it to us."

"We wouldn't dream of getting in your way," Frank said. "Do they know if Scott's going to make it?"

"They're not sure. He lost a lot of blood. We have a good trauma team at the hospital, though. If he's got any chance, I'm sure they'll pull him through. Now tell me about . . ."

Frank and Joe recounted most of the events that had occurred since they'd arrived at the village the day before.

The officer continued to question them for about forty-five minutes. Haddad frowned when they told him about the accident at the longhouse and the attack on Chet. "Why didn't you call the police?" he asked.

"With everything that's happened, we haven't had time to follow up yet," Frank said.

"Anyway, Mr. Trudson said the camp usually solves its own problems," Joe added.

"That's really up to the police to decide," Officer Haddad said, making a few notes in his book. "Especially if there's an ax murderer running around out here. I'll have to have a word with Mr. Trudson about that."

After Officer Haddad finished interviewing them, the Hardys decided to stop by the hospital to see how Scott was doing. The drive to Burton took about twenty minutes.

"Man, this is really a small town," Frank said as he looked up from the map he had been using to direct Joe to Burton. The main street consisted of two restaurants, a combination newsstand and bookstore, a hardware store, a market, and three bars.

"It shouldn't be too hard to find the hospital, then," Joe said, pulling into a gas station.

The attendant gave them directions, and a few minutes later Joe pulled the van into a space in the visitors' parking area of the hospital. He and Frank went straight to the main desk.

"We'd like to find out how Scott Thompkins is doing," Frank said to the woman there.

She checked the computer. "He's still in surgery," she said.

"Can we wait until he comes out?" Joe asked.

"Certainly," she said. "There's a cafeteria right down the hall, if you want to get coffee or something to eat. Feel free to check back a little later, say in an hour."

The Hardys went to the cafeteria, had something to eat, then returned to the front desk.

The woman checked the computer again.

"Good news," she said. "He's out of surgery and in the recovery room."

"What floor is he on?" Joe asked.

"He's on three, but he can't have visitors in the recovery room. If you check back later, I'll let you know when he's moved to a room."

"Thanks," Joe said. He and Frank turned away from the desk.

"We have to talk to him," Frank said quietly.

"I know," Joe said. "Follow my lead. I have a plan." He led Frank toward the hospital gift shop, which they had passed on their way to the cafeteria. They bought some flowers, then found the stairs.

When they reached the third floor, Frank hung back out of view. Joe sauntered up to the desk nurse. She was an attractive woman in her late twenties with dark hair and glasses. Joe quickly read her name tag.

"Evelyn," he said, "I'm supposed to deliver this bouquet to someone on this floor. The problem is, I dropped the card, and I can't remember who the order is for. But if you told me the name, I know I'd remember it."

"Flowers aren't usually delivered to his floor," the nurse said, "since these are the post-op recovery rooms."

Joe gave her his most charming smile. "Look, I need your help," he said. "If I don't deliver these flowers, I may lose my job."

The nurse checked the ledger. "Could they be

for Julie Kendall? She's the gymnast who broke her leg at the state meet."

"No. That name's not familiar." Joe walked around the desk to look at the nurse's clipboard. He briefly glanced up at Frank, who'd nonchalantly walked out of the stairwell.

"Maybe you should let me take a look." He smiled and leaned over her shoulder. As he did so, he flashed five fingers and then three to Frank. Frank nodded, found directions to the room on a nearby sign, and headed toward room fifty-three. The last thing Frank heard was the nurse saying to Joe, "Have we met before?"

Frank found the room right away. He had to duck back around the corner as another, older nurse came out of the room. He waited until she was gone and then sneaked in.

Inside lay Scott Thompkins, looking to Frank like a high-tech mummy. His arm was bandaged, and an elastic bandage covered his chest and his injured arm—probably to keep Scott from moving his arm, Frank surmised. The teen had tubes attached to various parts of his body.

Frank walked over to Scott. "Hi. I'm Frank Hardy. Remember me?"

Scott looked at Frank with groggy, half-closed eyes. He nodded.

"Can you tell me who attacked you?" Frank asked.

"V-Viking . . ." Scott said weakly. "Viking with an ax."

"Did you recognize him?"

Scott shook his head and started to say something, but a voice from the door interrupted. "What are you doing here?"

Frank turned to discover the older nurse he'd avoided a few minutes earlier.

"I'm from the Viking Village newsletter," Frank said. "The folks over there wanted to know if he's okay."

"Well, he will be if you get out of here," the nurse said coldly. "No visitors are allowed on this floor."

Frank nodded, apologized, and slipped out the door. He saw that his brother was still chatting with the nurse named Evelyn. He caught Joe's eye and motioned toward the elevator.

"Look," Joe said to the nurse, "why don't you take the flowers? I'll go back to the shop, check the computer, and bring another bouquet back later, after the patient is out of the recovery room."

Evelyn's eyes lit up. "For me? Are you sure?"

Joe handed her the flowers. "There are plenty more where these came from," he said, and grinned. Then he turned and headed for the elevator.

"What did you say your name was?" the nurse called after Joe.

He turned and winked. "Think of me as your secret admirer," he said as the elevator doors opened and he and Frank got in.

"You really made her day," Frank said as they got out on the first floor.

"It was the least I could do after she helped us out. What did you find out?"

"Not much," Frank said as they walked down the corridor. "Scott told me he was attacked by a Viking."

"So we have a Viking attacker on our hands. The question is, who is it?" Joe said.

"And is it someone from the village or someone who's using the village as cover?" Frank said.

"We need some answers," Joe said. "Where should we start?"

"I say the police station," Frank said as they walked outside. "Officer Haddad seemed pretty sympathetic. Maybe we can get some more information out of him." The Hardys climbed into their van and headed toward the station, which they'd passed on the way to the hospital.

A few minutes later they pulled up outside police headquarters. The place was abuzz with activity. It seemed to Joe that half the Viking Village was passing in and out of the station. The Hardys spotted the red-haired Hank Walsh and Brandt Hill on their way out and Dave Chisholm heading in. Brandt sneered at them as they passed. The Hardys ignored him.

As they opened the front door they were nearly bowled over by Ronalda Pearl, who was storming out of the station, an angry expression on her face. Two steps behind her was Nick Osgood, the bird-watcher. Neither of them said a word or acknowledged the Hardys in any way.

"Well, excuse us, too," Joe said.

Frank watched as Ronalda Pearl got into a Mercedes and drove off. "Do you think she's involved in some kind of deal with Mr. Trudson?"

"Could be," Joe said. "Let's see what we can pick up." He and Frank went inside and quickly located Mark Haddad in the chaos.

"Officer Haddad," Frank called, "can we have a few moments of your time?"

"Just a sec," the officer said, handing some papers to a secretary. "What's up, guys?"

"That's what we were hoping you could tell us. Do you have any suspects yet?"

"We've got nothing *but* suspects." Then his smile turned to a frown. "Uh-oh, can't talk now."

The Hardys followed his gaze to where a short, impeccably dressed policewoman was exiting an office. "Mark," she said, her voice exuding authority, "stop the chitchat and get me that paperwork."

"I just handed it to Greta, Chief."

"Then get me a cup of coffee and the forensic reports."

"Yes, ma'am."

"Boy, she's tough," Joe whispered.

"Just on me," Officer Haddad replied. "She's my mother." He headed down the corridor to do as he was told.

"You two," Chief Haddad said, holding the Hardys with her green eyes. "Do I know you?"

"Frank and Joe Hardy, ma'am," Frank said.

"Ah, yes," she said, nodding. "I heard about you. Are my officers still questioning you?"

"No, ma'am," Joe said.

"Then you'll have to stop clogging up the corridors around here. We're busy today, and we don't need any amateur help. I'll call you if we do." She looked toward the exit.

Frank and Joe took the hint.

"Glad she's not *our* mom," Joe said as soon as they were out the door.

The Hardys were starting down the steps when a police car pulled up. Joe could see someone sitting stiffly in the back. Did they have a suspect? Joe wondered.

The officer yanked open the door, grabbed the person by the arm, and pulled him to his feet. He was a big guy, and he was wearing a Viking costume. As the arresting officer turned to march the man up the steps, the Hardys realized who it was: their friend Chet Morton.

Chapter 8

"FRANK, JOE, AM I GLAD to see you!" Chet said with relief as he passed the Hardys.

"Excuse me, Officer," Frank said, turning and following the cop and Chet back up the stairs, "why are you arresting him? What's the charge?"

"Sorry, fellas. You'll have to ask the chief about that. I've got to get this guy processed. Step back, please."

"Hang in there, Chet," called Joe. "And don't say anything until we've talked to the chief." Chet nodded as the officer took him inside.

Frank and Joe went directly to the chief's office, but she wasn't there. They asked a desk clerk, who said she was busy in the interview room. The Hardys decided to wait and sat down on a bench.

Half an hour later the chief came out. "Chief Haddad, may we have a word with you?" Frank asked.

The chief stopped just outside her office, her hand on the doorknob. "Again? I thought I told you boys to go home."

Officer Haddad stepped between his mother and the Hardys. "You heard the chief, guys. Move along now."

Joe leaned around him. "All we wanted to know is why you arrested our friend Chet," he said.

"Morton?" Chief Haddad said. "Nobody's arrested him—yet."

"Then what are you holding him for?" Frank asked.

The chief smiled slightly. "Are you boys lawyers now as well as detectives? We're investigating a serious crime, and he's a suspect."

"Chet couldn't have done it," Joe said. "He was in his cabin at the time."

"He had motive, means, and opportunity," Chief Haddad said flatly. "And we have only his word on his whereabouts. Everybody saw him come to the crime scene late. Mr. Morton fits the description Mr. Thompkins gave us when he came to just before he went into surgery. He said his attacker was a large man dressed as a Viking."

"There are an awful lot of Viking costumes in

the village," Joe said. "Dave Thompkins knows Chet pretty well. He didn't finger him, did he?"

"Not specifically."

"You mentioned motive, ma'am," Frank said. "What possible reason could Chet have for attacking Thompkins?"

"You gave us that information yourselves," the chief said. "Mr. Morton choked on a stone that belonged to Mr. Thompkins. Plus Mr. Morton was attacked previously by an unknown party.

"We think the incidents are related. A grudge is a powerful motive. There are farmers up here who hold a grudge for generations. And when they do go on the offensive, they use the weapons they know best.

"It's well known that your friend Chet Morton is handy with an ax, which is what we believe caused Mr. Thompkins's wounds. The ax attack could have been Mr. Morton's retaliation for the earlier incidents."

"But Chet's ax is blunt. And you didn't find any blood on it, did you?" Frank said.

"Nothing visible, but we're sending it out for forensic analysis. And there are plenty of other axes around the compound he could have used."

"What about that Viking who's been lurking in the woods?" Joe asked.

Chief Haddad laughed. "The only people who have seen that so-called ghost are a bunch of teenagers with overactive imaginations."

"Frank and I saw it," Joe said.

"My point exactly," said the chief.

"No offense," Frank said, "but it seems as if you've got a lot of speculation and some circumstantial evidence. You don't have anything solid to pin on Chet, though. I don't think you can hold him on that basis."

Chief Haddad frowned, obviously annoyed.

"He's right, Mom—er, Chief," interjected Officer Haddad, who was still standing nearby.

"I don't care if he *is* right. I won't have amateurs telling me how to do my job." She was silent for a moment. Finally she said, "I'm releasing him—for now. But he *must* stay in Viking Village. If he leaves, I'll toss him in jail so quickly it'll make his head spin. Understood?"

"Fair enough," Frank said.

"Yes, ma'am," Joe said.

A few minutes later Officer Haddad appeared with Chet following. As the Hardys led their friend to the front entrance, they ran into Claire, who was also leaving the police station.

"They didn't arrest you, too, did they?" Chet asked her.

"Oh, no. But they had plenty of questions. How's Scott? Have you heard?"

"He's in pretty rough shape," Frank said. He'd overheard two cops talking while they were waiting for Chief Haddad. "The doctors saved his arm, though, and they say he should be okay. Need a lift back to the village?"

Claire nodded. "Yes, thanks."

The four of them piled into the van and headed toward the Viking Village, stopping on the way to eat dinner. "I'm not eating that gruel again tonight," Joe said.

It was dark by the time they arrived at the village. The rain had stopped, and a full moon hung high above the treetops. A brisk wind blew patches of fog through the village like fleeting ghosts. Mist still clung to the houses and the boughs of the trees, giving the whole scene an eerie look.

They went to Chet's cabin first so he could settle into house arrest. Ingrid greeted them at the door.

"Chet, I was worried about you," she said, giving him a quick hug.

"No big deal," he said. "Just a case of mistaken identity."

"Joe, why don't you and I walk Claire back to her cabin?" Frank said.

"Do you think the attacker is still around?" Ingrid asked.

"You never can tell," Claire said. "I'd be happy for the company."

"Well, keep an eye out for old man Trudson," Ingrid said. "This thing has really put him on edge. There's no telling how much business he lost today."

"Maybe the publicity will do him some good," Joe said.

"Joe Hardy, what a terrible thing to say," Claire said.

Joe shrugged. "You know what they say: any publicity is good publicity."

"Let's go," Claire said, hooking a hand through the elbow of each Hardy.

They headed for the boardwalk. When they reached it, they turned toward Claire's cabin. The village was silent. They had just passed one of the guesthouses under construction when the Hardys spotted two men in the shadows. They were clearly arguing.

"Liar!" the first man yelled. With that, he took a swing at the second man. The first man was Ivar Trudson; Frank and Joe didn't recognize the other one. He took a step back to avoid Trudson's blow and aimed a punch of his own. Frank and Joe rushed forward to separate the two.

"Whoa, cut it out!" Joe said, barely avoiding being punched himself. He put his hands on Mr. Trudson's chest and moved him back.

"You stay out of this," Mr. Trudson said. "Smith's had this coming for a long time."

"I've had it coming?" the man called Smith shouted. "You're the one who started this." He seemed about to charge, but Frank held him back.

"You've had it in for me from the beginning," Mr. Trudson said. "Now you're trying to sabotage the village."

"You're just getting what you deserve," Smith said, pointing menacingly at Trudson. "Don't try to blame your troubles on me."

The Viking Village owner ignored him. "Well, your scheme won't work. I'm on to you. You'd better not show your face around here again." He turned and stalked off into the night.

"Okay, settle down," Frank said, letting go of the other man.

"Who are you, anyway?" the man asked. "And why are you poking your noses into our business?"

Frank held out his hand. "Frank and Joe Hardy. We're detectives. Who are you?"

The balding middle-aged man shook hands reluctantly. "I'm Tom Smith," he said. "I used to own this land. That lunatic bought it for a few pennies, and now he's making a fortune off it. I know he found that stone before I sold the place to him, and one day I'll be able to prove it. You can bet he's at the bottom of all this trouble."

With that, Smith turned and headed for the parking lot.

"What's the beef between those two?" Frank asked Claire as they resumed walking toward her cabin.

"Well, as Mr. Smith said, this land used to be his farm. Five years ago he sold it to Trudson for practically nothing. I guess Mr. Trudson found the rune stone just after he bought the place."

"Smith seems to think Trudson knew about the stone *before* they closed the deal," Joe said.

"Maybe. Mr. Smith's been complaining for a long time about how Mr. Trudson cheated him," said Claire.

"How come you know so much?" Joe asked, looking down at Claire.

She smiled at him. "I've worked here for three seasons, longer than anyone but Dave Chisholm. I've picked up a thing or two."

They passed through the berm and into the staff lodging area. Lights were on in a few cabins, but the compound was very quiet.

"How long has the village been open?" Frank said.

"Four years. Dave's been here since the start."

"Maybe we should ask him a few questions," Joe said.

"That'll be easy enough. His cabin is almost next to mine. In fact, that's it right up ahead." She indicated a cabin with the lights out. "Looks as if they're asleep."

Frank peered into the darkness and cocked his head. His keen ears picked up sounds from inside the cabin. "But there's someone rummaging around inside," he said quietly. "You two stay here, I'm going to take a look." Frank hurried over, took a quick look in the window, and was back in less than thirty seconds.

"The place has been ransacked," Frank whispered. "Someone's in there all right. Sounds like he's still working it over."

"Let's take him," Joe whispered back. "Claire, you wait here."

The brothers rushed the cabin and burst through the door, but their quarry reacted instantly. Before the Hardys' eyes could adjust to the darkness, the person dived out the window.

Chapter 9

JOE JUMPED OUT the window after the intruder. "Frank, circle around!" he yelled.

"Claire, go inside and wait for us," Frank said as he ducked past Claire and skirted the cabin.

The intruder dashed through the fog toward the opening in the earthen wall that led to the main area. He was tall and thin and fast, but the Hardys were faster. Joe caught up to him just as he passed through the berm.

"Gotcha," Joe said, tackling the man by the ankles. The intruder went down, falling into a mud puddle. Joe flipped the guy over by his shirt and cocked his fist back to punch him.

"All right, I give up. Don't hit me," the man pleaded.

"Hank Walsh!" Frank exclaimed. "What are you up to?"

Walsh's expression changed from fear to annoyance. "That's what I should be asking you. What were you doing bursting into my cabin?"

"Your cabin?" Joe said. "I thought it was Dave Chisholm's."

"It's mine, too," Hank Walsh said. "We're roommates."

"What were you doing ransacking your own room, then?" Joe asked. "And why did you run away?"

Hank relaxed. "Dave and I were in town tonight. After we talked to the cops, we had dinner. We came back and found the place wrecked. Dave thought he saw someone outside and went to investigate. I was going to call the cops, but then I spotted you at the window. I thought you might have wrecked the place and then decided to come back, so I hid. Or tried to hide, anyway. Then you burst in, and I tried to get away."

Frank frowned. The story didn't quite ring true. "Where'd Dave go?"

"Last I saw, he was headed for the longship dock," Hank said.

Frank and Joe looked in that direction. They could just make out the dock through the swirling mist. Moonlight fell on the ship, and a breeze billowed the tent that stood on its stern. The boat rocked in the choppy waters of the lake. There was no sign of anyone near it.

"It doesn't look as if anyone's there now," Frank said, helping Hank to his feet. "Come on. Let's go back to the cabin. I want to check out your story."

"What's there to check out?" Hank asked.

"Just move it," Joe said, prodding him.

They met Claire at the cabin door. She'd turned on the lights.

"This place is a mess," she said. "Is that you, Hank? What were you doing wrecking your own place?"

Hank scowled at her. "I was just telling these guys—"

"So he does live here?" Joe interrupted.

"That's right," Claire said. "He and Dave are roommates."

"Like I told you," Hank said.

"Hey, sorry we roughed you up," Frank said. "And sorry about your place. Maybe whoever did this left some evidence."

All four of them went inside, and the Hardys started to search the place.

"Joe, take a look at this," Frank said after a few minutes. Joe went over, and Frank showed him where one of the hut's main support posts had been partially sawed through.

"A small-toothed saw," Frank said. "Just like the one somebody used on the longhouse frame."

"Looks like somebody didn't have time to finish the job this time," Joe said.

"You're right," Frank said. "And it's a good

thing, because someone could have been seriously hurt." He looked at his brother. "I don't think the collapse of the longhouse was meant to hurt us. I think we were just in the wrong place at the wrong time. But this"—he looked up at the post—"was a deliberate attempt to hurt somebody. Looks as if the saboteur's moving up from vandalism to endangerment."

Joe nodded in agreement. "And I have a hunch that the saboteur is also the Viking attacker."

Claire was examining several of the items strewn around the floor. "Look," she said. "This is some of the stuff that was stolen from the exhibits."

Joe came over to her. "What stuff?"

She picked up several items. "This brooch and these pieces of metal. They're supposedly from Viking spears. And these small carved stones."

"They look like the stone that Chet choked on," Joe said.

Frank crouched down to get a better look. "What do you know about this?" he asked Hank.

"I've never seen that stuff before," Hank said. He looked at the pieces. "They don't look like real Viking artifacts to me, anyway. Probably just more of Mr. Trudson's fakes. Or maybe something from the gift shop. This whole place is a historical scam."

"If you really think this place is crooked," Joe

said, "maybe it's time to put your money where your mouth is and talk to the police."

Hank frowned but didn't say anything. Then he changed the subject. "I'm really getting worried about Dave. He should have been back by now."

Frank stood up. "We'll check it out," he said. He turned to Claire. "You two call the cops and then wait here. Joe and I will come back as soon as we can."

The Hardys left the cabin and jogged toward the lake. Soon the longship dock came into view.

The wind blew wisps of mist across the lake, and the water was still choppy. The big boat rocked, creaking and banging up against the dock and throwing strange moving shadows all around. It was easily sixty feet long, Frank estimated, with high sides and a tall mast amidships. A tent had been erected in the stern section, just in front of the huge steering tiller. He assumed the tent was meant to protect the Viking explorers from the elements at sea.

"That's a pretty impressive replica," Joe said softly.

Shields hung over the oar holes, and the high prow and stern of the boat were carved to resemble the head and tail of a dragon. "It looks like something out of an adventure movie."

"It really does," Frank agreed. "Maybe Chet can take us aboard tomorrow. But for now we'd better get to work. You take the dock. I'll scout the shore," Frank said.

"Okay," Joe said.

Frank quickly found what he was looking for along the shore. "There are some tracks in the mud over here," he said. "Looks like there may have been a scuffle. You see anything?"

There was no answer.

"Joe?" Frank called when he didn't see his brother on the dock.

"Over here," Joe called softly and waved from the stern of the boat. He turned and exclaimed, "Frank, there's a body in the tent!" Joe could see a man's legs and feet protruding at an odd angle from underneath the tent.

Frank sprinted toward the dock. He waited for the ship to rock toward the dock, then quickly grabbed the handholds and scrambled aboard. He hurried past the rowing benches toward the stern. The ship's oars were piled neatly by the benches, ready for use. The wind gusted, tugging at the boat's moorings as he passed the square-rigged mast.

Though the longship's draft was shallow enough so that it could be beached during raiding forays, its gunwales were tall enough to protect the crew from the pounding seas. Standing amidships, he found it difficult to see over the sides.

Frank stared down at the legs. "Let's take a look," he said, and the Hardys ducked into the tent.

The man lay on his stomach, so they couldn't see who he was. The boat's rocking made it difficult to tell if he was breathing.

Frank and Joe knelt down to check out the body.

"Look at that lump on the back of his head," Joe said.

Frank felt for the carotid artery in the man's neck. "His pulse is strong, though," he said. "Let's turn him over. But be careful of his head."

They gently rolled the man on his back.

"It's Dave Chisholm!" Joe exclaimed. "So Walsh was telling the truth about him coming out here."

"Looks that way," Frank said, standing up and steadying himself against a tent pole. "We'd better call an ambulance."

"It may not be necessary. I think he's coming around."

Dave groaned, and suddenly his eyes popped open. He seemed disoriented, confused; he clearly didn't know where he was. He stood up and lunged forward, either to get away from Frank or to grab him. Then he grasped at the side of the tent, and his weight brought it crashing down on their heads.

Frank and Joe struggled under the heavy cloth, trying to avoid Dave's flailing arms. "Dave, snap out of it," Joe said. "It's us, Frank and Joe Hardy."

For a few seconds Dave kept flailing, pulling

one of the tent's mooring ropes in and further entangling them.

As Frank scrambled to find the edge of the fabric Joe grabbed Dave's arm and dragged him out from under the tent. The longship rocked, and Dave slammed against the side of the boat, then fell back, stunned.

Seconds later his eyes cleared, and he shook his head. He tried to get up, but he lost his balance and fell down again. Joe threw the tent off himself and helped Dave sit down on one of the benches.

"Oh, man," Dave said. "Sorry. I thought you guys were someone else."

"No harm done," Frank said. "Dave, any idea what happened? Who knocked you out?"

"It was that bird-watcher who's been hanging around. Nick Osgood, I think his name is. We've seen him lurking around camp for the last couple of weeks. Some people think he's pretty spooky. Guess they were right. Oh, man, my head hurts."

"Take it easy," Joe said, sitting down across from Dave. Frank took a seat on the bench beside his brother. "Just sit back and tell us everything you remember," Joe said.

Dave Chisholm blinked and stretched his neck. "Yeah. Okay. Hank and I came back to find our place wrecked. I saw someone outside and went after him. I caught Osgood on the beach. We struggled. You wouldn't know it to look at him, but that guy's tough. I remember he got me around the neck and knocked me to the ground. I must have hit my head on a rock 'cause everything went black. I guess he dumped me in the boat after he knocked me out." Dave paused and took a deep breath. He looked at Frank, then at Joe. "You think Osgood could be the one behind all this?"

"Might be," Frank said. "He looks like a strong suspect at this point."

"Do you think he's the Viking?" Dave asked, leaning forward and rubbing the back of his head.

"Possibly," Joe said. "And if he is, you're lucky you didn't get hurt worse."

"My head doesn't feel very lucky." Dave groaned again, then straightened. He looked past Frank and Joe, toward the bow of the ship. "Hey, guys, your lantern fell over," he said.

"What lantern?" asked Joe. He and Frank turned simultaneously.

In the bow, lying on its side on one of the benches, was a propane lantern. The Hardys could hear from the hiss that it was turned on. It wasn't burning, but a short rag, stuffed into it, was.

The brothers got to their feet, but the second they did, the boat rocked, knocking the lantern off the bench. As it hit the deck, the lantern shattered and immediately exploded into flames.

Chapter 10

"QUICK, ONTO THE DOCK!" Frank said as the explosion spread burning fuel across the wooden deck.

They helped the still-groggy Dave to his feet, steadying themselves against the rocking of the boat. As they struggled with their footing, some of the oars caught fire, and the flames spread into the rigging. The Hardys pulled Dave over to the gunwale.

"Uh-oh," said Joe, looking over the side of the longship. "We're in big trouble." The burning longship was no longer tied to the dock. It was drifting loose on Lake Superior, hundreds of yards from shore. "Somebody must have cut the boat loose while we were in the tent, trying to revive Dave."

"Yeah," Frank added, "and planted the burning lamp for good measure." He looked at the fire spreading toward them. "We've got to get off the ship or we're toast."

"How?" Dave asked.

"Let's put out the fire," Joe said, "and then row back to shore."

"No way," said Frank. "This ship's too big for the three of us to row. Besides, the fire's too far advanced. We'll have to swim for it."

"This water's freezing, even in summer," Dave said.

"You got a better idea?" Frank asked.

Dave was hanging back, so Frank took him by one arm, Joe grabbed the other, and they shouted "Geronimo!" in unison as they leaped off the burning boat.

Hitting the water was like getting a cold slap in the face. Joe broke the surface first and gasped for air. He'd lost his grip on Dave and looked around frantically for him and Frank. Seconds later Frank struggled to the surface with Dave, who was thrashing around, in tow.

Frank and Joe kicked hard to put some distance between them and the burning boat. The combination of the cold water and their saturated clothes made it slow going, however. Joe pulled off his sneakers to swim better, then tied the laces together and hung them around his neck.

"You need any help?" Joe called to his brother.

"Yeah," Frank said. Still groggy, Dave was deadweight. Frank was having trouble supporting him.

Joe swam to his brother's side. "Dave, just relax," he said. "We're not going to let you drown."

Frank took off his sneakers, tied them, and hung them around his neck, just as Joe had done. Then together the two Hardys slowly towed Dave toward the shore, using rescue swimming techniques.

Mist clung to the surface of the lake, making it difficult at times to see where they were going. The choppy water and wind gusts didn't make things any easier. Fortunately, both Hardys had an excellent sense of direction.

Finally they dragged themselves ashore near the dock. All three collapsed, trying to catch their breath. Frank noticed that Dave looked sick. The cold swim hadn't done him any good, he thought. Out on the lake, the longship consumed itself in a fiery Viking funeral.

"Talk about going out in a blaze of glory," Joe said. He noticed that the mooring line, which had held the ship to the dock, had been cut. "Clever. Whoever it was pushed us out on the lake while we were struggling with Dave."

Frank watched as the last embers of the burning boat started to break up and slip beneath the waves. "That was close," he said, pulling his wet sneakers on again. "Give me a minute to catch my breath, and then we can head back to camp."

He lay down on his back and took several deep breaths. As he relaxed for a moment, he caught a glint of moonlight off something in the woods.

"You okay, Dave?" Joe asked as he put on his sneakers.

"B-been better." Chisholm was shaking, and his lips were turning blue.

"We'd better get you to someplace warm," Joe said.

Frank slowly got to his feet, still focusing his attention on the woods. "You guys do that," he said. Yes. He was sure of it now. The moon was reflecting off glass—or glasses. He was fairly certain someone was watching them with binoculars.

Frank took off.

"What's wrong? Where are you going?" Joe called after his brother.

"Somebody's watching us. I'm going to find out who. Get some help for Dave."

"Watch yourself," Joe called. "It could be the same guy who set that lantern-bomb."

"That's what I'm hoping," Frank said over his shoulder. He sprinted up the hill and into the woods where he'd seen the reflection.

His quick action paid off. A dark shape sprang up near the edge of the woods and took off in the opposite direction.

Frank dug down deep into his energy reserves, pushing his chilled legs as fast as they would go. His wet sneakers sloshed on the pine needles.

The watcher dodged between the pines, but Frank was determined not to let him get away.

The man crossed a small clearing, and Frank caught a brief glimpse of him in the moonlight. It was Nick Osgood. Frank smiled grimly. It looked as if he'd found the attacker. Now all he had to do was catch him.

Joe helped Dave Chisholm to his feet, and together they made their way back toward his cabin, with Dave leaning heavily on the younger Hardy.

"Man, I would have been a goner without you guys. How'd you know where to find me?" he asked weakly.

"Hank told us you'd followed the guy who ransacked your place. He said you were headed for the dock. Unfortunately, we didn't believe him at first. We checked out the cabin, then decided to take a look down at the dock."

Dave nodded. "Lucky for me you did."

"There's one thing that I don't get: if Osgood was behind all this, why was that stolen loot in your room?" Joe asked.

"What are you talking about? There was loot in my room?" Dave asked. "What kind?"

"A lot of small stuff that Claire said was missing from the exhibits. Any idea how it got into your cabin?"

Dave shrugged. He seemed to be regaining his strength. "Beats me. Maybe Osgood dropped the stuff when we caught him snooping around. Or maybe he put it there on purpose. Somebody's obviously stirring up trouble around here. Maybe he was trying to frame Hank or me for the theft."

"Why would he do that?"

"I don't know," Dave said. "Why did he attack me? Why'd he bust up my place? Why did he do any of this stuff?"

Meanwhile, Frank was asking himself the same questions. Nick Osgood's pace hadn't slackened. He was obviously in top shape—at least a lot better than your average bird-watcher. Frank knew that normally he could have caught the guy, but after his cold swim, it was all he could do to keep up. Plus Osgood obviously knew the woods better than Frank did.

Frank was so caught up in his thoughts that he almost didn't notice the trip wire in front of him. Fortunately a shaft of moonlight glinted off the wire. Frank's quick reflexes paid off, and he pulled up just short of the trap.

Now, who put this here? he wondered. He paused a minute and looked around carefully. He couldn't see any other traps in the area.

Thinking about it, Frank decided Osgood might have deliberately led him in this direction. Did the bird-watcher know about the wire? Was this a trap?

A large, dark shape rested against a nearby tree. Frank squinted, trying to make out what it was. It looked like a tent, he thought, or a lean-to of some kind.

As Frank peered into the darkness, Osgood jumped him from behind.

Frank couldn't believe he'd been so careless. He hadn't seen the bird-watcher double back, and now he was fighting off a blind-side attack.

Osgood threw an arm around Frank's neck, trying to choke him. Frank jammed his elbow backward toward Osgood's stomach, but caught him only a glancing blow. The two struggled, their feet shuffling through pine needles and leaves in a macabre dance.

Frank felt his leg brush up against something. It was the trip wire.

Frank heaved himself to one side, away from the wire, but Osgood didn't let go. Instead, he tightened his grip around Frank's neck.

"This is the last time you'll stick your nose in my business, boy," the bird-watcher hissed.

Frank grabbed Osgood's arm with both hands, hoping to loosen the choke hold with a judo throw, but Osgood had obviously had some martial arts training; he countered the move expertly.

Frank's limbs felt like lead, and the pressure around his neck was beginning to make him woozy.

Osgood tried to force Frank to his knees. Frank knew he was finished if the man succeeded, for Osgood would then be able to use his weight to apply more pressure to the choke hold. He'd be able to cut off Frank's air completely.

Desperately, Frank tried to hook his toes around Osgood's ankle and trip him. It almost worked. The two of them stumbled backward.

Then Frank felt the trip wire go taut around his ankle. Osgood grunted, his breath hot on the back of Frank's neck.

Out of options, Frank stomped down on Osgood's toe as hard as he could. To Frank's surprise, the trip wire snapped—and to his horror he saw a bent sapling with a long hunting knife attached to the end of it whipping directly toward his chest.

Chapter 11

FRANK'S FOOT-STOMP caused Osgood to relax his grip ever so slightly. At the last instant Frank broke free and ducked sideways. The knife whipped past him and hit the startled bird-watcher with a thud. Osgood's eyes went wide with shock, and he fell back, dead, the knife embedded in his chest.

Frank slumped to his knees, his breath coming in heavy gasps. He hadn't meant for it to end like this. What a horrible way to go.

"I'm sick of waiting," Joe said. "The police should be here by now."

"You know it takes at least fifteen minutes to get here from town, even if you break every speed limit in the books," Claire said.

"Well, when they show up, tell them I went to find my brother." With that, Joe grabbed a flashlight and jogged off into the night.

It didn't take him long to locate Frank. As he chased Osgood, Frank had left a clear trail through the woods.

Joe spotted the body and then his brother. "Oh, man, are you okay?" he asked.

"Yeah," said Frank. He'd built a small campfire by the lean-to and was sitting on the ground flipping through some papers and notebooks.

"What happened?"

"Somebody set a trap, and Nick Osgood got caught in it."

"That's awful," Joe said.

"Awful for him," Frank said, "but lucky for me." He looked up at his brother with a slight smile. "He was trying to kill me at the time."

"Something tells me he was into more than just bird-watching."

"Brilliant deduction," Frank said. "Are the cops on their way?"

"Yep. Claire called them." Joe put his hand on his brother's shoulder. "Burglary and vandalism—that's one thing, but an attempted murder . . ."

"Well, it's murder, now," Frank said. "Whoever set this trap knew it could kill someone."

"Osgood may have set it himself," Joe said.

Frank nodded, then paused to listen. "I think I hear sirens. Why don't you go get the cops? I'll stay here and keep checking through Osgood's stuff. Once the police get here, they'll pack up everything as evidence."

"Sure thing," Joe said. "I'll be right back."

It took several hours to sort everything out. The police cordoned off the area, took Osgood's body away, and started a thorough search for evidence. They also detained Frank and Joe for questioning, and by the time they had finished giving all their answers, the Hardys were completely exhausted.

"I think we've got the man behind our mini-crime wave," Officer Haddad said. "Or what's left of him anyway. Good work, guys. Mom—er, the chief—will be impressed by your work."

"I'm just glad it's over," Joe said.

Suddenly Ivar Trudson stormed up to them, hair flying, a wild look in his eyes. "You're right that it's over!" he shouted. "Ever since you've been here snooping around, things have gotten worse." He motioned toward the lake. "Now, because of you, my longship's been destroyed. My insurance won't begin to cover the loss. What are you trying to do, ruin me?"

He reached out as if to grab Joe by the neck, but Officer Haddad stepped between the two. "Calm down, Mr. Trudson," he said. "The Hardys had nothing to do with the ship being destroyed. I suspect that Osgood set the fire to get rid of Dave Chisholm—although I don't know why he'd want to kill him."

"But—but—" Mr. Trudson sputtered.

"Mr. Trudson," Officer Haddad said, "it's late. I suggest you get some sleep." He turned to the Hardys. "And you two should get some rest as well. But remind your friend Chet Morton that he has to hang around until we formally clear him, which shouldn't take long."

"Will do," Frank said. After saying good night to the police officer, the Hardys headed toward Chet's cabin, anxious to get away from Mr. Trudson.

Chet was fast asleep when they arrived, and the Hardys quickly got undressed and settled into their beds.

"You know, Joe," Frank said as he adjusted his pillow under his head, "somehow I don't think this case is wrapped up."

"What do you mean?"

"Well, I got a chance to look through Osgood's stuff before the police arrived. He had a diary."

"And . . . ?"

"From what I could tell, he wasn't interested in sabotaging the camp. He started out just scouting the place, making a log of what he saw and when."

"Like he was investigating something?"

"Right—or someone. But pretty soon the tone changed. He didn't seem to be interested in spying anymore. The later entries were concerned with finding a Viking treasure he thought was buried around here."

Joe yawned. "A treasure? What do you think about that?"

Frank yawned, too. "I'm too tired to think right now. Ask me in the morning."

It was well past noon when the Hardys finally awoke to a bright, clear day, Chet had already left for work. They dressed, went to the dining hall, and had a quick bite to eat.

Afterward they checked the forge and found Chet hard at work as a Viking blacksmith.

"Chet, got a minute?" Frank asked.

Chet put down the hammer and tongs he was working with and wiped the sweat from his forehead. "Sure. I tried to wake you guys up for breakfast, but you were both out like lights. I was wondering why until I overheard Hank at breakfast talking about what had happened last night. To hear him tell it, it was like a war zone out there." Chet stretched. "Sounds like you guys had a busy night. I sacked out right after Ingrid went home." Chet smiled at his friends. "Guess the troubles are over. The police cleared me, right?"

Frank frowned. "Not officially, but Officer Haddad said they should soon. As for the trouble being over, there are still a few things that don't add up."

Joe picked up his brother's thought. "Chet, what do you know about some kind of Viking treasure rumored to be in the area?"

"Viking treasure? I've never heard of it. Where did you guys get that?"

"I read it in Osgood's notes," Frank said.

"You might check with Dave or Claire," Chet said. "They've worked here the longest. If anybody knows about a treasure, they would. You could talk to Mr. Trudson, too, I guess. But he's not exactly receptive to rumors."

"And he's been so pleasant and outgoing lately," Frank said. Joe and Chet chuckled. "Come on, Joe. We'll catch you later, Chet."

"Stay out of trouble," Joe said.

Chet waved. "Hey, with you guys on the case, it's only a matter of time."

"Where to?" Joe asked his brother when they were outside.

"Osgood left the police station last night with Ronalda Pearl, right?" Frank said.

"Right," Joe said. "The woman Trudson was arguing with." He looked at his brother. "Are you thinking what I'm thinking?"

"Probably," Frank said. "I thought we might pay her a little visit and see if there's any connection."

Joe grinned. "My thought, exactly."

The Hardys found Ronalda Pearl in the phone book, and soon they were in the van on their way to her house. It was a twenty-minute drive from Viking Village. When they got there, they saw a police car pulling out of the driveway. Frank pulled the van over to the curb. They waited a few moments, then got out and walked up to the house. Joe knocked on the door.

The woman who greeted them at the door was not the same well-dressed, in-control businesswoman they'd seen before. Ronalda Pearl looked as if she hadn't slept, and it was clear she'd been crying.

"Ms. Pearl, I'm Frank Hardy, and this is my brother, Joe. We're investigating some of the trouble at Viking Village, and we'd like to ask you a few questions."

"Can't it wait?" she said wearily. "I'm exhausted. Are you with the police? The rest of your unit just left."

"No," Joe said, "we're freelance detectives. Officer Mark Haddad will vouch for us. A friend of ours might be charged with attempted murder. We think you could clear some of this up. We won't take too much of your time."

She sighed. "All right. I know Haddad and his mother. But if this is some kind of trick, I should warn you that this house has surveillance systems and silent alarms." She opened the door and led the teens inside.

Ronalda Pearl's house wasn't quite a mansion, Joe thought, but it was a far cry from Viking Village.

She led Frank and Joe through several rooms with cathedral ceilings and into a small study. There she sat down in a leather chair behind a mahogany desk and nervously lit a cigarette. She motioned for Frank and Joe to take the two chairs across the desk from her.

"The first thing I want you to know," she said between puffs, "is that I never intended for any of this to happen when I hired Nick Osgood. I don't know exactly what he did, but he wasn't doing what I was paying him to do."

"What had you hired him to do?" Frank asked.

She sighed and blew a smoke ring. "It'll be in the papers tomorrow. And since I already told the police, I might as well tell you."

"It can't hurt, and it might help our friend," Joe said. "What's the connection between you, Osgood, and what's been going on at the camp? And why were you arguing with Ivar Trudson the other night?"

"Ivar and I are *always* arguing. It's our way. I hold the papers on Viking Village."

"Loan papers?" Frank asked.

"Yes. He couldn't get a loan from any bank, so he came to me. I'm pretty big in local real estate, so I was a logical choice. I rounded up a small group of investors for him. Since I put up the largest percentage of the money, I'm the one with the most say.

"We think that Viking Village could be a major hit, even if the rune stone turns out to be a fake." She stubbed out her cigarette and lit another one. "The problem is, Ivar's stubborn. He doesn't want to do anything that might compromise the historical accuracy of the place.

You wouldn't believe the trouble I had just getting him to build a gift shop. Honestly, I almost think he doesn't want to make any money."

"Go on," Frank said.

"Anyway, that's what we were arguing about. I wanted more entertainment, like the mock battles, and more luxurious rooms for the guests. He wants to give people the experience of being 'real Vikings.'

"Unfortunately, he's not making enough money doing it his way. He hasn't finished building a single guest lodge—luxurious or simple—and his loan is coming due. I can't hold off the other investors forever. I was trying to persuade him either to commercialize the property or sell the whole thing to me. I could turn that place around in six months."

"So what did Nick Osgood have to do with all this?" Joe asked.

"Ivar was digging his heels in. I—I needed something to make him change his mind. Osgood is . . . I mean, *was*"—she stopped and wiped her eyes— "a private investigator. I hired him to spy on Ivar, see if he could dig up any dirt."

"But he ended up sabotaging the place," Frank said.

Obviously agitated, she stood up and began pacing. "If he did, it wasn't on my instruction," she said. "You think I'd destroy my own investment?" She waved the smoke away from her face agitatedly. Then, regaining control, she sat down again. "I don't know *what* Nick was up to, really. All I know is that I hired him to do one thing, but he seemed to have his own agenda." She leaned back in her chair.

"In any case, I'm out of it now. Ivar can default on the loan for all I care. It's not worth my getting mixed up in this mess any further."

Frank leaned forward. "Tell us what you know about the Viking treasure."

She chuckled. "That old rumor? There's nothing to it. It's just something made up by the kids who work in the village. Gives them something to occupy their minds when they're not working."

"Do you think Osgood was the one running around the woods dressed as a Viking?" Joe asked.

She sat up with a start, almost dropping her cigarette. "No. Wearing a costume wasn't Nick's style. I always figured that was some harebrained prank of Ivar's to drum up publicity. 'See the wild Vikings in their natural habitat,' or something."

"Publicity usually doesn't include attacking other employees with an ax," Frank said.

"No, it doesn't," she agreed, stubbing out her cigarette. She leaned back in her chair and closed her eyes. "Now, if you boys don't have any more questions, I'd like to get some rest. You can see yourselves out."

As soon as they were out the door, Joe turned to his brother. "Boy, people like her really burn me up," he said. "She hired Osgood, but she doesn't want to take responsibility for anything he did. It's like she pointed a cannon at the village, and now that it's gone off, she claims she didn't know it was loaded."

Frank hopped into the driver's side of their van. "We'll just have to let the cops handle her," he said. "I'm sure they'll be looking into her background to see if she's done anything illegal. She did seem pretty shook up, though. Sounds to me like maybe Osgood was just a loose cannon after all."

Joe got in the passenger side and buckled up. "If the cops can prove he was the one who attacked Scott and Chet, we can go back on vacation."

Frank started the van and pulled away from the curb. "Let's hope so."

The Hardys spent the twenty-minute drive going over the case again.

As Frank drove through the woods that were part of the Viking Village, he said, "Maybe the police will turn up some more clues in Osgood's diary. I wish I'd had more time to examine it."

"Maybe he just went nuts thinking about that mythical treasure," Joe said. "Stranger things have been known to happen." Suddenly Joe's eyes widened.

"Frank, watch it!" he yelled as a huge man in a Viking costume dashed into the road in front of the van.

Chapter 12

FRANK HIT THE BRAKES and yanked the wheel hard to the right. The van skidded onto the shoulder of the road, just missing the fleeing figure.

"Hang on!" Frank said as the tires hit a patch of mud on the shoulder and the van fishtailed. He fought hard to regain control, spinning the wheel in the other direction, but the van lurched off the road and down into an overgrown culvert, finally bumping to a stop, its front wheels embedded in a gully at the bottom. Frank and Joe unbuckled their seat belts and jumped out.

"I'm not going to let him get away this time," Joe muttered, bounding up the slope of the culvert.

"Are you up for some exercise?" Frank asked, sprinting after his brother.

"Sure, but no more cold-water swimming," Joe said. He dashed across the road to where they'd last seen the Viking. The younger Hardy quickly spotted some tracks leading uphill into the woods.

"This way!" Joe called, taking off.

Frank followed hot on his brother's heels. "Do you see him?" he asked.

"Not yet, I . . . Wait. There he is."

A short distance ahead, Frank could make out a large figure crouching behind some undergrowth. As the Hardys rushed him, the Viking took off farther into the woods. Frank saw that he was carrying a large ax.

The man set a brutal pace, dodging the pine trees with what appeared to be practiced ease.

"Looks pretty spry for a dead man," Joe said.

"Yeah. I guess that blows the Osgood-did-everything theory."

"Do you think the van's okay?"

"Sure," Frank said. "I don't think anyone's going to get it out of the ditch except a tow-truck driver."

As they ran, the woods grew denser and there were outcroppings of boulders, making the going more difficult.

The Viking easily dodged the rocks in his path. Ahead, Joe heard the sound of rushing water. "Maybe that river will slow him down," he said.

However, the Viking didn't stop when he reached the bank of the river. The water level was very low at that point, and the man bounded across a few slick rocks—as if he were playing a child's stepping-stone game, Joe thought.

Joe and Frank tried to do the same, but Joe nearly lost his footing on the third rock out. "Whoa," he said, pulling up. "This is tricky."

Frank helped steady his brother, working hard to keep his own footing. "Yeah. We'd better take this slow. Stopping for a quick dip won't help us catch him."

Joe looked downriver. "That guy must know this area like the back of his hand. This looks like the river that comes out north of the village."

"Probably," Frank said, picking his way across the rocks more carefully now. "But it has to go a long way downhill before it gets there." They'd been climbing steadily ever since they got out of the van. Frank figured they must be at least a hundred and fifty feet above the level of the road now.

"Come on," Joe said as they reached the far side of the river. He started to run again but caught his foot in a hole on the bank and went sprawling forward onto his face.

Frank, who was just behind Joe, stopped. "You okay?"

Joe lurched to his feet and winced. "I twisted my ankle, but don't let me slow you down. Just get him."

It took Frank a few moments to spot the Viking again. The man had built up a good lead, and

Frank bore down, concentrating on closing the gap. He heard pine needles crunching behind him and glanced back to make sure it was only Joe. He saw that his brother was keeping up pretty well despite the twisted ankle.

"Way to go, Joe," Frank said as they ran.

"Nothing hurt but my pride." Joe smiled, but Frank could see it in his brother's face: he was straining. Frank was feeling it, too. The events of the past few days were catching up with them. His breathing was labored, and beads of sweat built up on his forehead and trickled down into his eyes.

Then, just when Frank thought they were about to lose the Viking, he stopped, turned, and charged.

"Iiiieeeeaaaaa!" The Viking's war cry split the still air. He brandished the huge ax above his head, his massive arms barely straining with the weight, his well-muscled legs pounding the earth like big pistons. The man's blond hair and long, full beard waved wildly, and his blue eyes, barely visible under the visor of his iron helmet, blazed with lust for combat as he charged.

"Look out!" Joe yelled to his brother.

The Viking charged between them and aimed the ax at Frank's head. Frank ducked—just in time.

As the Viking lumbered past them, Joe kicked him hard in the back. The Viking staggered forward but caught himself against the trunk of a tree. He turned and snarled at the brothers.

Frank looked at Joe. This wasn't the time to stand and fight. "Let's get out of here," he said.

They both took off as the Viking charged again, screaming.

The Viking's ax whizzed through the air over Joe's head, embedding itself in a tree in front of them. Before Frank could stop him, Joe turned and charged the Viking. He planted his shoulder solidly in the stomach of the giant, but it was like hitting a wall. The Viking seized Joe by the shirt and flung him into a nearby boulder. Joe hit the rock with a dull thud, then slumped to the ground.

Frank lashed out with a martial arts kick. The Viking blocked the blow with both hands, lifting Frank into the air and sending him sprawling on his face. As they pulled themselves off the ground, the Hardys looked at each other.

"Should we split up?" Joe said.

Frank nodded, and they took off in opposite directions. The tactic confused the Viking for a beat. He went back to the tree and yanked out his ax before starting after Joe.

The Hardys executed a slant-in football pattern and reunited several hundred yards later.

"He's pretty solid for a ghost," Frank said.

"Way too solid," Joe said. "The guy's built like a cement truck."

They came to an abrupt halt at the riverbank.

The river was wider here, with a swift-moving current.

"Whoa!" Frank said, pulling up just in time.

"We can't cross here," Joe said. He eyed the far side, gauging the distance at about thirty-five feet. "Where are those stepping-stones?"

Frank glanced in both directions. "Upstream, I think."

"Can we make it?"

The brothers glanced behind them. The Viking was closing in fast.

Frank and Joe realized they were trapped. They'd hit the river at a bad bend. The Viking could cut them off if they tried to run either upriver or down. They didn't have a lot of options.

"I really didn't want to go swimming again today," Frank said.

"Me neither," Joe said as they scrambled down the riverbank and leaped into the icy water.

Frank surfaced and shook the water from his hair. "Man, it's cold."

"I noticed," Joe said as the current quickly carried them downstream.

The Viking crashed through the underbrush at the river's edge and raged at them. He snatched up a few rocks and threw them at the brothers, but he didn't follow them into the water.

"Guess it's not time for his monthly bath," Joe said. He ducked as a rock flew over his head and sank with a splash. "Ugly cuss, isn't he?"

Frank took a good look at the Viking, memorizing the man's wild features. "Swim for the other side, Joe."

"Right."

The Hardys struck out for the opposite bank, but the current made the going difficult.

Joe felt as if he were swimming in place. Suddenly he heard a roaring sound. "Hey, Frank," he gasped, "do you hear that?"

Frank shook the water from his ears and listened. "Waterfall!" he yelled.

They could both see it now—a raging cataract that plunged over the edge of a cliff just ahead. And they were caught in the powerful current, headed straight for it.

Chapter 13

"QUICK," FRANK SAID. "That tree over there."

Joe looked to where his brother was pointing. A large pine tree with a long, bare trunk hung out over the river on the far side, just before the waterfall. They swam hard for it, struggling against the current.

"The tree's too high!" Joe shouted over the roar of the falls.

"Not if you give me a boost. The current may be strong, but fortunately the river's not too deep."

"All right, here goes," Joe said.

Frank got in front of Joe and put his feet in his brother's hands. Joe bobbed underwater, and when his toes hit the river bottom, he planted his feet and then flung Frank upward with all his might.

Frank jumped off Joe's springboard and reached up high to grasp the tree trunk. He knew that everything depended on the next few seconds. With great effort, Frank pulled himself up and wrapped his body around the trunk. Then, with one arm around the trunk, he reached down with the other. "Grab my hand!" he shouted.

Joe reached up, but the current carried him away. He kicked hard and managed to swim back again. He reached up and felt Frank's hand.

Frank lashed backward with his legs as Joe drifted away. Joe kicked harder and flailed wildly with his hands. He found the tops of Frank's sneakers, grabbed on, slipped his fingers in the laces, and held on tight.

Frank grunted as Joe's weight threatened to drag him off the trunk, which creaked under their weight.

"Think it'll hold?" Joe asked.

"It better. Hang on." Slowly Frank pulled until Joe could reach up and grab the tree with his other hand.

Once Joe was safely sitting on the long trunk of the tree, he asked, "Now what?"

"We back down very slowly," Frank said, "until we hit the bank."

A few minutes later they reached the edge of the riverbank, and they both collapsed.

"I don't ever want to do that again," Frank said, gasping for breath.

"Me neither," Joe said. "Any sign of our friend?"

Frank looked around. The Viking was nowhere to be seen. "No. I guess he didn't think it was worth swimming across the river to nab us."

"Either that or he thought we were goners."

"Frank," Joe said after he had caught his breath, "did that Viking remind you of anyone?"

"Well, his costume looked like the one Chet wears, but now that you mention it, he did look like—"

"Ivar Trudson. With a fright wig and beard."

"Right, so what do you figure . . . ?"

"I'm thinking maybe Tom Smith was right and that Trudson's looking to drum up publicity for the village by dressing up and acting like a madman."

"That would be pretty extreme," Frank said, leaning back on his elbows. "He could have killed us."

"Well, maybe he's a Jekyll-and-Hyde type—a real nut. Chet said he's been acting weird lately. He does seem pretty tightly wound. And some people will do anything for a buck."

"It's worth checking out," Frank said, getting to his feet. "Let's get out of these wet clothes and see if we can find Trudson."

They picked their way downhill past the falls, which emptied into a clear, deep pool. Then the river continued on, but with fewer rapids. The

Hardys followed it to where it ran into Lake Superior, a half mile north of the Viking Village.

From there they hiked out to the main road and back to their van. As they approached, they saw a blue pickup parked by the ditch. Someone was checking out the van.

"Hold it," Joe called out and jogged over. "What are you doing over there?"

Tom Smith climbed up out of the ditch. "This is your van?" he asked. "I was driving by and saw it in the culvert. Thought somebody might have been hurt."

Frank crossed the road to talk to him. "No. We're fine, thanks."

Mr. Smith eyed the teens suspiciously. "Looks like you been swimming. You're on my property, you know. Do you mind telling me exactly what you're up to?"

"We ran off the road to avoid hitting a guy dressed as a Viking," said Joe.

Mr. Smith frowned. "One of Trudson's rowdies, eh?"

"No," Frank said. "It wasn't one of the village workers. This guy tried to kill us with an ax, and we had to jump into the river to get away."

Mr. Smith crossed his arms over his chest and looked skeptical. "You'll have a hard time convincing me that anybody dressed as a Viking 'round here isn't part of that crowd. I'm half convinced you boys are here just to stir up trouble yourselves."

"If you help us tow our van out of this ditch," Joe said, "we'll be happy to get out of here and never come back."

"That's the best offer I've had all day," the man said. "You boys got some rope?"

"It's in the van," Joe said, scrambling down to retrieve it.

It took about fifteen minutes for the Hardys and Mr. Smith to rig the rope and haul the van out with the farmer's pickup. They thanked him and got back on the road.

Night was falling by the time they reached the village. They stopped briefly at Chet's cabin to change. He wasn't there, so they left a note on his pillow and went to Mr. Trudson's office. It was closed.

Joe checked his watch. It was still running despite a thorough dunking in the river. "Everybody's probably in the great hall having dinner."

"I could use something to eat," Frank said. "Let's go."

The hall teemed with staff, but there were no guests. "Boy," said Joe, looking around the hall, "word must have gotten out that the village isn't such a safe place anymore."

"Yeah," Frank agreed. "By the looks of the staff, they're not too thrilled about being here, either." The usually boisterous staff members were talking quietly, and no one looked very cheerful.

The Hardys spotted Claire Benson, Hank Walsh,

and Brandt Hill sitting in a corner of the room talking quietly. Even Brandt seemed unusually sedate, Frank thought. He hardly gave the brothers a second glance as they entered the room. Claire waved curtly at them, then went back to her conversation.

Mr. Trudson sat eating at a table not too far from his workers. The Hardys made their way across the hall to him.

"Sir, we need a word with you," Frank said.

"About a little incident this afternoon," Joe said.

"What do you mean?" Mr. Trudson asked. He put down his bowl and scowled at the teens. "I thought you were leaving today."

Frank could see his brother's temper rising.

"We'll be glad to leave," Joe said. "As soon as we find out who the Viking was who chased us through the woods and tried to kill us with an ax."

Trudson gave Joe a strange look. "Of course you're joking."

Joe was getting really angry now. His voice rose. "The guy who chased us looked exactly like you in full Viking battle dress."

Ivar Trudson narrowed his eyes and stared at Joe. "I don't know what you're talking about. I've been right here in the dining hall for the past three hours."

Claire piped up from the nearby table. "That's right. He's been here since late afternoon."

Everyone else in the hall had turned to watch the confrontation.

Frank started to put his arm on Joe's shoulder, but it was too late.

Joe stepped forward and grabbed Ivar Trudson by the front of his shirt. "Why don't you come clean before someone else gets hurt—or killed? How far will you go for a little publicity? Are you that desperate?"

Still sitting, Trudson yanked his shirt from Joe's grip. For a moment he seemed ready to punch Joe, but then he caught himself. "I told you before—*get out of my camp!*" he shouted. "If you're not gone by morning, I'll have you both arrested."

With that, Trudson stood and stormed out of the hall. Everyone in the place sat in shocked silence.

Joe turned to his brother. "Why'd you let him go, Frank? He's in this up to his bald spot."

"Probably. But we don't have any real proof. What got into you, Joe?"

"I'm just tired of this. There's a maniac loose around here, and nobody's doing anything about it."

"I know," Frank said. Then his eyes narrowed, and he stepped forward. Something on the floor had caught his eye, and he bent down and picked it up. It was a small silver cross on a chain. The chain was attached to the bottom of the cross rather than the top.

"What's that?" Joe asked.

"An upside-down cross," Frank said. "It must have fallen off Trudson when you grabbed him."

Suddenly Frank's face lit up. "Wait a minute . . . I know what this is. How could I have missed it?"

Most of the people in the hall had returned to their dinner. Claire, Brandt Hill, and some of the other workers were still huddled around a nearby table talking quietly among themselves. Frank crossed the room and showed the pendant to Claire.

"Claire, what is this?" he asked.

"It's a Thor's hammer, obviously," she said. "Sacred to the Vikings. Are you guys nuts? I thought Trudson was going to deck you both. What's going on?"

"Tell you later," Frank said, pulling Joe to one side.

"So it's not a cross?" Joe asked.

"No," Frank said. "It's a Thor's hammer, an ancient Viking religious symbol."

"I just realized that's the same symbol as on Chet's lucky ring," Joe said. "So maybe this little trinket is part of the so-called Viking treasure."

"Maybe yes, maybe no," Frank said. "But I'm willing to bet someone thinks it is."

"That ring could be why Chet was jumped," Joe said. "Remember, the guy grabbed him around the throat? Suppose the attacker was trying to get the ring, not just choke him."

"Makes sense to me," Frank said. He turned back to Claire and the others. "Have you guys seen any other stuff with this symbol?"

"You mean aside from in the gift shop or display cases?" Claire asked.

"I found some stuff down by the river once," Brandt said quietly. He stared resolutely into his mug. "A couple of stones and a small piece of metal. One of the stones had that symbol on it. Mr. Trudson confiscated them when he found out I had them."

"Could they have been part of the Viking treasure?" Joe asked.

Brandt took a drink from his mug. "What treasure?" He turned and looked at Joe out of the corner of his eye.

Claire rolled her eyes. "That old rumor? Don't tell me you guys fell for it. That's for the tourists—something to keep the paying customers interested."

"No," Frank said. "We don't believe it. But we're checking a few things out."

"You'll have to do it quick, since you have to get out of camp by tomorrow," Brandt said, glaring at Joe.

"I'm not too worried about that," said Frank. "Any of you guys seen Chet around?"

They all shook their heads. Brandt scowled.

"I think he had an early dinner," Claire said. "I didn't serve his table, but I thought I saw him earlier."

"Let's go see if we can find him," Frank said to Joe. They turned and left the dining hall together, heading for Chet's cabin.

They didn't see Chet, or anyone else, on their way back to the cabin. The entire village looked deserted. Chet's hut was empty when they arrived.

"That's strange," Frank said. "The cops told him not to leave. I can't believe he wouldn't have stuck around to tell us if they cleared him."

"Maybe he's with Ingrid," Joe said.

"Let's check her cabin."

"I want to grab my jacket first," Joe said.

Joe went out to the clothesline, but his letter jacket wasn't there. "Now, where could it have gotten to?" he said, wandering back inside.

"Here it is," Frank said. "I found it lying on the foot of your bed. Chet must have taken it in when it dried." He handed the jacket to his brother.

As Joe slipped the jacket on, a piece of folded white paper fell out of the sleeve.

Joe picked up the paper, unfolded it, and started to read. As he did, his eyes widened, and he exclaimed, "I don't believe this!"

Chapter 14

"WHAT IS IT?" Frank asked.

"According to this, Ingrid's been kidnapped."

"Kidnapped?" Frank repeated. "Let me see." He read the paper over his brother's shoulder.

The message was plain enough: "If you want to see Ingrid again, wait by the rec room phone for instructions."

It was printed in block letters. There were four other words scrawled on the paper as well: "Longship dock" and "Bring ring." Frank and Joe immediately recognized the scrawl.

"That's Chet's writing," Joe said.

"He must have waited for the call, got his instructions, and gone to meet the kidnapper. He left the note so we could follow him. I just wish he hadn't tried to handle this alone."

"Well, what are we waiting for?" Joe asked. They raced down to the dock, but there was no sign of Chet.

Frank checked around and found a spot where the dirt and sand had been kicked up. "Looks like signs of a struggle," he said.

"I guess this is a popular place for fights," Joe said. He peered into the woods.

"That makes sense," Frank said. "It's far enough from the main buildings not to be easily seen."

"But close to the woods," Joe added, "which makes for a quick getaway."

"If only we hadn't been attacked by that Viking, we might have been here when Chet got the note," Frank said.

Joe nodded. "And it looks as if you were right about the treasure being behind this. Chet's notes said to bring the ring. Obviously he meant the ring he was wearing on the chain around his neck—the one he found."

Frank thought for a minute. "If only we knew where Chet found that ring, we'd have someplace to start searching."

"Wait a minute," Joe said. "Didn't Chet say something about that in his letter?"

Frank snapped his fingers. "That's right!" The letter Chet had sent with his hand-drawn map was still in the van. "If we can read it through my coffee stains, we're in luck. Tell you what, you go get the letter. I'm going to give Scott Thompkins a call."

"What for?"

"He had that carved stone that Chet almost choked on. Those trinkets may belong to the Viking, or they could be part of the treasure. Either way, if we can figure out where they came from, maybe we can track Chet or some of these other people down."

"Makes sense to me," said Joe. "Let's go to it."

Frank hurried over to the rec room phone, and the hospital put him through to Scott Thompkins's room.

"Hello?" a sleepy voice on the other end said.

"Scott? This is Frank Hardy—Chet Morton's friend. Remember me? I need to ask you a few questions."

"Okay."

"That small stone of yours, the one that turned up in Chet's food. Where did you find it?"

"Um . . ."

"Look, this is really important. It may be a life-and-death situation."

"I—um—found it on the riverbank, about a half mile upstream from the mouth."

Frank did some quick thinking. "You were over there when the Viking attacked you, too. What were you doing? You were supposed to be working on the farm."

"I—uh . . ."

Suddenly it all fell into place for Frank. "You were looking for the treasure, weren't you?"

There was silence on the other end of the line. Finally Scott said, "Oh, man, I knew someone else would figure it out eventually. You guessed it—I was poking around for the treasure when that maniac attacked me. I've been looking for it off and on for the last two summers. The only thing I found was that stone."

"Did you put it in Chet's food?"

"Huh? No way. Why would I do that?"

The note of surprise in Scott's voice sounded genuine to Frank. "I don't know," Frank said, "but I figured I'd ask. Thanks for everything. You've been very helpful. For what it's worth, I believe you."

"Hey, one more thing before you hang up . . ." Scott said.

Frank thought he sounded a lot more alert than when they'd started the conversation. "What?"

"If you do find that treasure, make sure I get some credit, okay?"

"Don't worry," Frank said. "I'm sure you'll get what's coming to you."

Scott laughed weakly. "I think I already did."

As soon as he and Frank split up, Joe headed for the staff parking lot. He ran into Brandt Hill coming from the opposite direction. Brandt was dressed in his Viking costume and carrying his war hammer.

Joe got ready for action. "If you're looking to pick up where we left off, I'm game," he said.

But Brandt raised his hands, palms open, letting the weapon slip to his side. "Hold on," he said. "I'm not looking for any trouble."

Joe relaxed slightly. "What a surprise."

"Look," Brandt said, "I got another lecture from the boss this morning. One more screwup and I'm out of here. He's dead serious. He also threatened to press charges if I get into any more fights. I don't figure that you, Chet, and Ingrid are worth that kind of trouble. This job may pay crummy, but it beats Hamburger World or the county jail."

"So you're going to leave Chet and Ingrid alone?"

"Morton's a loser anyhow. Ingrid will figure that out and come around. She was my girl once, and she will be again."

"And you'll stay out of my way, too?" Joe asked, genuinely surprised.

"I don't have a problem with you," Brandt said. "I realized I was out of line when they questioned me at the police station. That was a scary thing that happened to Scott. And then that bird-watcher getting killed, you know. . . . A lot of weird stuff has been going on around here lately. No way I want to be involved in any of it. I just want to do my job and collect my check."

Joe extended his hand. "Sounds like a good idea. No hard feelings, then."

Brandt and Joe shook hands. "No hard feelings." Brandt turned and continued on his way. "Hope you square things with Mr. Trudson."

"Don't worry," Joe said. "We won't leave without taking care of that."

Joe shook his head as Brandt walked away. It was amazing how a run-in with the cops and a dressing-down from the boss could change a guy's attitude. Joe hoped the change was permanent.

Joe continued on to the staff parking lot. He found the van at the far end, unlocked it, and hopped in. He pulled Chet's letter from the glove compartment where Frank had stashed it. He glanced at the letter; it was still legible through the coffee stains. He pocketed it, jumped out of the van, and locked up.

On his way back across the lot, he spotted Hank Walsh rummaging through the trunk of a car. Hank had the spare tire compartment lid raised. Did he have a flat? Joe couldn't see one from where he was standing.

Still, it looked as though Hank might be having a hard time. Maybe his jack was stuck. Joe turned in the redheaded man's direction.

"Hey there," he called out. "Need any help?"

Hank barely glanced at Joe. "No," he said, then quickly slammed the compartment lid down.

"You sure?" Joe asked, walking toward the car.

Hank turned and leaned against the trunk, blocking Joe's view of the inside. He had a strange expression on his face. Something clearly was wrong, Joe thought.

"No," Hank said. "I told you, nothing's wrong."

"Look," Joe insisted, "I'm sure I can give you a hand." He wanted to see what was in the trunk. As Joe stepped forward to get a better look, Hank reared back and swung at Joe.

Chapter 15

JOE DUCKED and Hank's blow missed him. By sheer reflex, he counterpunched, and his fist landed squarely on Hank's jaw. Hank's head snapped back, and he slumped to the ground, unconscious.

What's going on here? Joe wondered, scratching his head. He picked up Hank off the pavement and propped him against the car in a sitting position. Then he took a look in the trunk. Beneath the half-closed tire compartment lid, he spotted something.

He took a handkerchief from his pocket, reached in, and pulled out a foot-long collapsible saw. The teeth were small and close together. Tiny chips of wood still clung to the blade.

"Hey, Joe, what's going on?" It was Frank, back from his phone call to the hospital.

"That's just what I was asking myself," Joe said. "I'm not sure, but old Hank here took a swing at me."

Frank looked at Hank; he was just beginning to stir. "Looks like he'll know better next time. Any idea why he took a poke at you?"

"Not really. But I did find this in the trunk." Joe held up the saw.

Frank whistled. "Attaboy. Just like the one that cut through the main timber in the long-house frame."

"*And* the post in Hank and Dave Chisholm's cabin."

Joe pulled Hank off the ground and twisted his arm behind his back. "Let go," Hank said groggily. "That hurts."

"Whose car is this, and what were you up to?" Frank asked.

"It's my car, and none of your business," Hank said, struggling to break free.

"This saw makes it *police* business," Frank said. "Do you want us to call them now, or are you going to come clean first?"

Hank stopped squirming. "Look. It's not my saw. It belongs to my roommate, Dave Chisholm."

"Oh?" Joe said, giving Hank's arm a sharp twist. "What's it doing in your car, then?"

"Dave's my friend. I found the saw in our room. I didn't want him to get into any trouble, so I decided to hide it."

"That doesn't wash," Frank said as he started

searching through the trunk. "I'm remembering when you put down the village in front of Joe. We heard you do that a lot."

"You seem to have some grudge against this place," Joe said. "Maybe enough of a grudge that you'd commit sabotage."

"No. You've got it wrong, I—"

"Hey, Joe, look what I found here." Frank held a letter in his hands. The envelope had been addressed but not sealed or stamped. "It was inside a book." He started to skim the letter.

"Interesting reading?" Joe asked, making sure to keep a firm grip on Hank's arm.

"It's a letter to Hank's graduate adviser. Seems his master's degree is hanging on discrediting this place—or, more specifically, the rune stone. I quote, 'My personal experience indicates that the Viking Village proprietor is a publicity seeker, not someone with a real interest in science. This can be demonstrated by the recent spectacular events that have occurred at the camp. I have no doubt that when I finally get to examine the stone, it will prove to be a fake.'

"He continues, 'Thus there is no need for further delay in approval of my thesis. I look forward to finishing up the process this fall. Yours sincerely, Hank P. Walsh.' "

Frank glared at Hank. "Looks as if you do have an ax to grind. Maybe you were running around the village swinging one at people, too."

"You don't seriously think I'm this Viking nut," Hank said.

Frank kept glaring at Hank but gave Joe a wink on the side.

"You have access to the weapons and costumes," Joe said. "You've got plenty to gain if the village fails. That's motive and opportunity." Joe started pushing Hank back toward the village. "Come on, Hank. You've got some explaining to do—to the cops."

Hank dragged his feet. "Hey, I just pulled a few pranks, no big deal. Nobody was supposed to get hurt," he said. "I swear I'm not the Viking."

Frank grabbed him by the collar and looked him in the eye. "Prove it. We've found you with the saw. Your letter proves you have a motive. We could go straight to the cops with all this. If you don't tell us what's going on, we'll make sure they go hard on you."

Hank turned pale. "Trudson doesn't deserve to succeed. He's built this place on a scam. My thesis proves that the Vikings didn't get any farther than Nova Scotia. Any Norse items this deep in North America are merely goods they traded with the American Indians. Trudson's rune stone is a fake. I could prove it if he'd let me near the thing."

"So you sabotaged the new longhouse that nearly brained Joe and me," Frank said.

"Okay, but I never intended for the frame to

fall on anybody. It was just supposed to collapse."

"Why did you cut the beam in your own hut—to divert suspicion from yourself?" Joe said as he pushed Hank toward the dining hall.

"Yes," Hank said. "I planned to 'discover' the sabotage later. Nobody would think I did it to my own hut. But I never got to finish it."

"Where does Dave fit in?" Frank asked.

"He's up to something, but I don't know what," Hank said. "I'm pretty sure he stole those artifacts you found in our room. I caught him looking at one once, when I came back from work early. I didn't think much of it at the time, but when you guys found the stuff, I realized what it was. Since you weren't buying my story, I thought I could blame him."

"So Dave's not working with you?" Frank said.

Hank looked nervously at Frank. "No. I'm on my own. None of these dweebs had any clue to what I was doing."

"What about the Viking? What do you know about him?" Frank asked.

"Nothing. I told you, I was working alone. I never meant for anyone to get hurt. That Viking's probably a publicity stunt gone berserk."

"One last question before we turn you over to the cops," Joe said. "Where's Chet?"

"What are you talking about?"

"Chet's missing, and it looks as if Ingrid's been kidnapped."

Hank looked genuinely surprised. "I don't know anything about it. Honest."

The Hardys found John, the security man, resting near the gate and turned Hank over to him. They gave John instructions to call the police and to hold Hank until they arrived. Then they found a quiet place near the camp entrance, and Joe pulled Chet's letter out of his pocket.

"I didn't have a chance to reread it before," Joe said, unfolding the letter and holding it in the light from a nearby window. "Let's see. . . . Chet says here that he found the ring while swimming in the pool at the bottom of the falls. That must be the same falls we almost went over."

"Scott said he found his artifact by the riverbank," Frank said. "He was looking for more treasure near there when the Viking attacked him."

"And Brandt said he'd found some artifacts by the river mouth," Joe said, "which means they came from the pool or upstream somewhere. I'll bet the Viking's hiding out somewhere in that area."

"Let's grab our flashlights from the van and start searching," Frank said.

Fifteen minutes later Frank and Joe were headed upstream from the mouth of the river. They moved quickly, surveying the ground with their flashlights and keeping an eye out for the Viking.

"Who do you think that guy is?" Joe asked.

"I still think he could be someone hired for a publicity stunt. But maybe he's another treasure hunter who doesn't want people on his turf."

They continued to search, and after about ten minutes Joe said, "Look, tracks." He pointed to the ground in front of him where his flashlight clearly illuminated several footprints.

Frank bent low to examine the marks, comparing them to his sneakers. "They look like size twelves. It could be Chet," he said. "And there's another set, which probably belong to the kidnapper."

"Or the Viking," Joe said.

They followed the tracks upstream until they neared the pool. Then Frank stopped.

"Lights out," he whispered. They both clicked their flashlights off.

As their eyes adjusted to the darkness, they could see a dim glow coming from behind the waterfall, about fifteen feet above where it emptied into the pool.

"There must be a cave up there," Joe said.

Frank nodded. "Looks like someone's inside."

"Time to get wet again," Joe said. He and Frank quickly stripped to the waist and stepped into the chilly water. They waded out until the water in the pond reached their chests and then swam toward the falls. Joe held his flashlight in his mouth, trying to keep it out of the water.

Frank stuck his hand into the waterfall. The pressure was heavy, but with their rock-climbing experience, he figured they could handle it. Carefully feeling for his grip, he inched his way up the cliff face. Joe followed.

When he got about twelve feet up, Frank's hand found open air. "It's a cave all right," he whispered. "More of a tunnel, really. Let's see where it goes." He hoisted himself up through the opening, and Joe followed.

The walls of the tunnel were slick with water. The Hardys could hear voices up ahead.

"Man, I can't believe it. What am I gonna do with you now?" said one voice.

"Well, for starters you could untie me." Joe and Frank both recognized the second voice—Chet's.

"I can't do that. Don't you understand? You know about this place now. You know about the treasure."

"I wouldn't if you had let Ingrid go," Chet said.

"I know you were looking for the treasure. That's why you kept that ring a secret. You had to be close to finding it. With the police and everybody poking around, someone was bound to find it soon. I had to find out what you knew."

The Hardys crept forward quietly.

"I don't care about any treasure. Where's Ingrid?" Chet asked angrily.

The other voice let out a nervous laugh. "Too bad you woke up."

"Pardon me for having a hard head," Chet said.

Frank poked his head around the corner of the tunnel and saw a large cave. Joe peeked around the corner, too.

The kidnapper stood in the middle of the cavern holding an ax handle. The room was large, with several smaller passages leading from it. The roar of the falls echoed through the chamber. A small lantern in the center of the cavern provided light. Chet was tied to a stalagmite nearby.

"I've been searching for this treasure for four years," the kidnapper said. "It's just not fair after all this work."

"Life's not fair, Dave," Frank said, stepping around the corner and into the firelight.

Dave Chisholm spun around at the sound of Frank's voice, but the brothers were already on him.

"Good timing, guys," Chet said.

Dave Chisholm sidestepped Joe's tackle and, wielding the ax handle like a club, hit Joe on the back. But that set Dave up for Frank, who spun into him with a hard right, catching him flush on the side of the head.

As Dave staggered back, Joe rolled to his left, kicking Dave in the knees. He pitched forward, and Frank caught Dave's weapon in his left hand, then pounded his face again with a solid right. Blood trickled from Dave's nose, and he collapsed face-first onto the ground. Joe quickly grabbed him in a full nelson.

"Nice work," Chet said, squirming in his ropes.

"Guess that about wraps it up," Joe said.

"Not so fast," said a familiar voice from one of the side tunnels. A shadowy figure pointing a gun emerged from the darkness.

Chapter 16

AS THE FIGURE came into view, they saw that it was Ingrid Lampford.

"Let him go," she said, gesturing toward Dave Chisholm. *"Now."*

Joe released his hold on Dave.

"Ingrid, what are you doing?" Chet asked.

"Shut up, Chet," Ingrid said. She waved her gun at the Hardys. "The two of you, up against the wall next to your friend. Move it."

"But why?" Chet asked.

"Dave and I have been working together since the beginning to find the Viking treasure," Ingrid said. "We've actually known each other for years. We've been going together since we were freshmen in high school."

"Then you were just playing up to Chet to find out about his ring," Joe said.

She smiled again. "Just like I did with Brandt. Chet was harder, though. He never wanted to talk about himself, never mind where he'd found some silly old ring. Such a modest guy."

"So when we first met you, you were actually searching Chet's room," Frank said.

Ingrid smiled. "You almost caught me at Scott's, too, but I slipped away before anybody saw me." She turned to Chet. "Sorry, but I'm afraid it's over between us."

Chet's face reddened. "You—you—" he sputtered. "I can't believe I fell for it."

"So you two were responsible for stealing all the artifacts and for breaking into people's cabins," Joe said, trying to edge toward where he'd put down his flashlight before tackling Dave. "And I bet it was Dave who mugged Chet that first time. You were trying to steal the ring, weren't you?"

Dave got to his feet, scooped up Joe's flashlight, and went to stand beside his girlfriend. "Brilliant deduction, Sherlock."

"And then you tried to brain us by toppling that tree on us," Frank added.

"I don't know what you're talking about," Dave said. "I didn't have anything to do with any tree falling."

He sounded as though he was telling the truth, Frank thought. And since he had admitted to one attack, it didn't make sense for him to deny the other.

"You put that stone in Chet's food, though," Joe said. "I guess you hoped if he choked, you could grab the ring."

Before Dave could answer, Ingrid laughed and said, "That's a good idea, but neither Dave nor I had anything to do with that, either. You guys must be accident-prone."

"Ingrid's right—it wasn't planned," Dave said. "I swiped the stone from Scott's room, and then I tried to pass it to Ingrid in the dining hall. But Scott almost saw me, and I had to dump the stone in the bowl. It was only dumb luck that you grabbed the bowl from me."

"Too bad you didn't choke, Chet," Ingrid said. "It would have saved me the trouble of shooting you now."

Frank and Joe exchanged a glace. They were too far away to jump Ingrid, and there was no good cover nearby. She raised her gun and took aim at Chet, but Dave grabbed her hand.

"Hold on, Ingrid," he said. "Killing people wasn't part of the plan."

"Sorry, Dave, but they know too much."

"Let's just tie them all up and leave them here. By the time anyone finds them, we'll be long gone."

"That's not a chance I'm willing to take."

Frank and Joe exchanged another glance. With

Ingrid and Dave arguing, this was their chance. Frank gave a slight nod.

"Look, these guys saved my life when the longship burned," Dave said. "Osgood almost killed me."

"Dave, listen to me," Ingrid said coldly. "The Hardys think they're some kind of detectives. They're big do-gooders, and they'll keep after us until we're rotting in jail. They've got to go."

Dave stepped back from Ingrid and shook his head in resignation. Frank tensed his legs for a final, desperate charge, but before he could jump, a deafening bellow filled the cavern and the Viking lumbered in from one of the side passages.

Ingrid spun around, leveling her gun at the intruder.

The Viking charged her, knocking Dave out of the way as if he were a rag doll. Dave banged his head against the wall and slumped to the floor. "Mine!" the Viking screamed. "Mine!"

The Viking swung his ax at Ingrid. She stepped back and pulled the trigger.

Blam! The shot echoed through the cavern, but the Viking kept coming at her.

She squeezed off two more shots, but the Viking didn't fall. Ingrid staggered back as he knocked the gun out of her hand and swung his ax wildly.

"No!" she screamed, stepping backward toward the opening to the falls. The Viking grabbed at her with one huge hand, but she stumbled, lost her footing, and toppled into the raging falls with another scream. "*Noooo . . . !*" The Viking slumped to his knees beside the opening as the rushing water quickly smothered Ingrid's cry.

"Talk about timing," Joe said.

Frank bent over the Viking. Even close up, he was a ringer for Ivar Trudson. "Can you talk?" he asked. "Who are you?"

The Viking's eyes rolled back in his head, and he passed out. He'd been shot in the chest, shoulder, and abdomen. "He's hurt bad," Frank said. "We have to get him out of here."

"Dave's just knocked out," Joe said. "He'll be fine. Think we can get them out through the waterfall?"

"No way," Frank said. "We can't carry them down that rock face."

"We didn't come in through the falls," Chet said. "There's another entrance."

"Show us," Frank said.

"Sure, but how about untying me first?"

Within seconds the Hardys had transferred the ropes from Chet to Dave. Using Joe's flashlight and the lantern, Chet led the group out through one of the side passages. Frank and Joe carried the Viking as carefully as they could, while Chet dragged Dave, who was groggy but conscious, by the ropes. Eventually they came to a concealed passageway between two boulders near the top of the falls.

"Hey, Chet, how'd you get caught in the first place?" Joe asked as they began to take their prisoners downhill toward the village.

"I got the note about Ingrid being kidnapped. I didn't want to wait for you guys to get back. So I took the phone call, left the note for you, and went to meet the kidnapper at the dock. Dave threatened to hurt Ingrid if I didn't tell him all about my ring." Chet gave his captive a nasty look, then continued. "So I did, and then he clocked me with that ax handle. He thought I was knocked out, but I was just stunned, and I followed him to the pool. I got there just in time to see him and Ingrid at the top of the falls.

"I followed them to the hidden tunnel entrance. They disappeared inside. Then someone hit me from behind, and I woke up tied to that rock."

"Dave must have gone into the cave, then come out the side entrance and clobbered you," Joe said. "The Viking knew about the side entrance, too. How's he doing, Frank?"

"Not too good. I don't think we should carry him any farther." Gently he and Joe laid the Viking down on the ground. "Chet, I want to check the bottom of the falls for Ingrid. Maybe you should—"

"What happened here?" The Hardys and Chet spun at the sound of Ivar Trudson's voice.

"Mr. Trudson," Joe said. "Who *is* this?"

Trudson knelt by the Viking's unmoving body

and cradled him gently in his arms. The resemblance between the two was remarkable.

The Viking's eyes flickered open. He smiled weakly. "P-protect the trove . . . whatever it takes. . . . Kill any intruders . . ." the Viking said through bloodstained lips. Then he passed out again.

Mr. Trudson whipped a cell phone out of his pants pocket. "John, this is Ivar. I'm near the bottom of the falls. Someone's been shot. I need an ambula— What? The police are there already?"

"We had John call them earlier," Frank said.

"Well, send them up right away with an ambulance." He hung up the phone.

"So," Frank said, putting a hand on Trudson's shoulder, "can you tell us about your connection to this man."

"He's my brother, Eric." Trudson took a deep breath and let it out slowly. "He's mentally unbalanced. I kept him in a private hospital for years. I couldn't afford it anymore, so I brought him here to live with me. In hindsight, I guess that was a bad move.

"Eric was always obsessed with our Norse heritage—far more even than I am. Out here I didn't think he could do anyone any harm. He used to roam the woods pretending he was a Viking. Sometimes I found trees almost chopped through or chopped down. I thought he might be planning to build a hut for himself. He told me once he was looking for a place to make his own secret outpost."

"I'd say he must have found that spot in the cave behind the falls," Joe said.

"There is a cave behind the falls?" Mr. Trudson said. "I never knew that. Well, that kind of place would have been perfect for him. And it explains why I couldn't find him when I went looking."

"So he was the ghost Viking all along," Chet said.

"That's right. I didn't think he could get violent until the attack on Scott Thompkins. Then I knew I had to do something. I've been looking for him ever since."

A few minutes later the police and the paramedics pulled up in two four-wheel-drive vehicles. Frank and Joe helped the medics stabilize Eric Trudson. Chet turned Dave Chisholm over to the police, who cuffed him and put him in the backseat of their car.

Officer Mark Haddad hopped out of one of the vehicles. "Well, the Hardys are here, so I guess we should expect trouble. What's going on?"

"It's a long story," Frank said. "But the bleeding guy is Mr. Trudson's brother. He's the one who attacked Scott Thompkins and who attacked us in the woods. Dave Chisholm, the guy who's tied up, is responsible for the thefts and some of the sabotage. Hank Walsh caused some problems, too."

"We've got him in custody already."

"Chisholm was working with Ingrid Lampford," Joe said. "She was fighting with the Viking. She shot him, and then she fell into the falls. I doubt she made it."

Officer Haddad signaled for two of the other officers. "Carl, Mike, check for a body at the bottom of the falls." The officers nodded and jogged off.

"We figured out from his notes that Osgood set the trap that killed him," Officer Haddad said. "He was trying to catch the Viking. He didn't want to kill him; he hoped to capture the Viking so he'd take him to the treasure. It was just bad luck he got nailed himself."

The medics quickly stabilized Eric Trudson and strapped him to a stretcher. As they slid him into the vehicle, he woke up and started to pull at his straps.

"Ivar," he called. "Ivar, promise me. Please stop anyone who finds the treasure. Protect it at all costs. Stop *them.*" He gestured wildly at Frank and Joe. "They're after us. I tried to stop them, but—"

"It's all right, Eric," Mr. Trudson said. "I won't let anyone steal our treasure."

"So," Chet said, "is there really any treasure or isn't there?"

"Let's see what Dave Chisholm knows," Frank said, walking to where the prisoner was waiting in the back of the police car. "Come on, Chisholm. Where's the treasure?"

Dave took a deep breath. "There is no treasure—aside from the artifacts in the Visitor Center. Scott and Brandt found a few stones by the river, and Chet found the ring. We took it away from him in the cave, but it turned out to be a ring that the gift store sold. All Ingrid and I ever found was an old pile of bones and some metal junk, back in one of the passages of the cave. I don't even remember which one."

"Let's go take a look," Joe said.

Joe and Frank led Chet, Officer Haddad, and Mr. Trudson back into the tunnels. When they reached the main cave, they fanned out, each taking a different passage.

A few minutes later everyone heard Joe's excited voice. "Over here, guys. This must be it."

They all hurried to join him and stood in a semicircle over a pile of bones and artifacts.

"It's junk, just as Dave said," Chet said.

"Hold on a minute," Mr. Trudson said, kneeling down to take a closer look. He carefully sifted through the pile for a few minutes, then picked up a large rusty chunk of curved metal. It was a helmet. "This is genuine Viking battle gear. And this is a brooch clasp," he said, holding up another rusty metal object. "I'm willing to bet these bones are the skeleton of a real Viking, which backs up all my claims that the Vikings really did settle here and that the stones weren't just carried here by Indians. If I can prove it, the village will finally make some money. I'll put Eric back in treatment, finish the buildings, and pay off my debts. Maybe I can even settle accounts with Tom Smith. The publicity from this discovery will make Viking Village a world-famous attraction."

"Well, in that case, you can hire some real Vikings to work here," Chet said, "because I quit.

"Way to go," Frank said softly.

Joe looked at his brother. "Now can we finally go on vacation?"

Frank and Joe's next case:

Frank and Joe have taken summer construction jobs in the Hell's Kitchen section of New York City, and they're feeling the heat. The site has been plagued with mishaps, and it's no accident. The Hardys have found plenty of criminal sleaze mixed in with the concrete, and it threatens to turn the future skyscraper into a forty-story disaster! Millions of dollars and untold lives hang in the balance as the boys seek out the source of corruption. Organized crime and hired thugs have already taken a hand, creating a blueprint for murder. But as the danger builds to a climax and the bullets begin to fly, Frank and Joe find that they could end up taking the biggest fall of all . . . in *Stress Point,* Case #125 in The Hardy Boys Casefiles™.